may be kept

SEVEN DAYS

charged for each day the book is kept overtime.

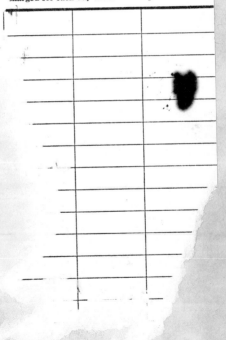

Me and
Mr. Stenner

Evan Hunter

This is for my daughter—
Amanda Eve Finley

1

Mr. Stenner didn't know what a Shirley Temple was.

I thought a grown man had to be pretty dumb not to know what a Shirley Temple was, but I didn't say anything about it. Mom smiled at him and said he certainly had a lot to learn about eleven-year-old girls, and then she told him what it was, and ordered one for me. I'll tell you the truth, I felt somewhat betrayed. It was my *father* who'd introduced me to Shirley Temples, which I used to ask him to order for me whenever we went out to eat. I didn't plan on sharing with Mr. Stenner anything Daddy and I had shared, and was in fact going to order a Coke. But Mom said, "Would you like a Shirley Temple, honey?" and that was when Mr. Stenner asked what a Shirley Temple was, and that started the whole dumb thing.

I sipped at the drink like a lady spy I'd seen on television, watching Mr. Stenner over the rim of the glass, ready to *do* something if he pulled a Luger pistol from his belt. Mr. Stenner seemed very nervous. Mom seemed nervous, too. I could tell; she was smiling a lot.

"Well, what do you feel like eating, Abby?" Mr. Stenner said. "They've got some very good steaks here, and if you care for seafood . . ."

"I'm not hungry," I said.

"They've got children's portions, if you . . ."

"No, thank you, I'm really not hungry."

"Maybe you'll change your mind," he said.

"Maybe," I said, and then picked up my straw and blew some bubbles into the Shirley Temple.

"Abby, please don't do that," my mother said.

Everyone was always telling me I looked just like my mother, with the same blue eyes and blond hair. My mother's hair was clipped short, though, and my own hair fell almost to the middle of my back, just like my Aunt Harriet's. Aunt Harriet was my father's sister. She lived in New Mexico. *She* had blond hair and blue eyes, too, and frankly I thought I resembled *her* more than I did Mom. Mom wore eyeglasses, for example. Aunt Harriet didn't. Nobody on my father's side of the family wore glasses, for that matter, and neither did I. At the table that night, I was the only one not wearing glasses. Mom was wearing glasses, and Mr. Stenner was also wearing glasses, and I remembered him having said they were aviator glasses, so I asked him if he was an aviator.

"Me?" he said, and laughed. "No, I'm not an aviator."

"What are you then?"

"You know what he is," my mother said, and smiled and looked at him across the table.

"No, I don't."

"He's a photographer."

"You mean you take pictures?"

"Yes," Mr. Stenner said.

"Movies?"

"No, stills."

"What's stills?" I asked.

"How would you define stills, Lillith?" Mr. Stenner said. "Let me see . . ."

I once looked up the name Lillith in my book of four thousand baby names. That was when I was hoping my mother would have another baby, and was looking up baby names all the time. In the baby-name book, it said that Lillith meant "evil woman" or "bad wife." I couldn't imagine why anybody in her right mind would give her daughter a name like *that*, so I asked Grandmother Lu if she knew what Lillith meant. Grandmother Lu said she didn't, and when I told her, she said, "Well, well." Grandmother's full name was Lucille, which in the baby-name book said "See Lucy," and Lucy was from the Latin for "light." Abigail was "a source of joy"—which wasn't bad.

". . . or newspapers or magazines, or even the family album. Those are all stills," Mr. Stenner said.

"Do *you* take pictures for magazines?" I asked.

"Yes, I do."

"What kind of pictures?"

"Fashion, mostly."

"Do you ever take pictures of animals?"

"I've taken pictures of animals, yes. But mostly I take pictures of people."

"What kind of animals?"

"Well, all kinds."

"Tigers?"

"No, I don't think I've ever . . ."

"You said all kinds. Do you take pictures of people playing tennis or swimming or . . . ?"

"No, most of my work is posed. Studio work, do you know what I mean?"

"Daddy has a studio, you know. He's an architect."

"Yes, I know."

"He designs industrial complexes," I said.

"Uh-huh," Mr. Stenner said.

"Not houses. Industrial complexes."

"Mm," Mr. Stenner said.

"Maybe he'll let you take a picture of something he designed."

"Maybe he will."

"Though I guess if Daddy wanted a picture taken, he'd take it himself," I said, and knew by the look my mother shot me that I'd made my point; what I was saying was that I didn't think much of Mr. Stenner's job. Mr. Stenner got the point, too. He suddenly looked very embarrassed and picked up his menu and began studying it.

I'm not really a brat, please understand that. But, you know, you come home from school one day, and you plunk your books down and go into the living room, and there's your mother wearing her Long Grave Face and sipping tea which she never brews except in times of national emergencies and certain disasters or calamities, and she tells you she's leaving your father, tells you in fact that your father has already taken a room at a hotel as a temporary measure, that you and she will soon be making other plans . . .

"Mr. Stenner," I said, "when Mommy and I move into the new house, will we own it?"

"No," he said, and put down the menu. "It'll be rented."

"Who'll be playing the rent? Daddy?"

"No," Mr. Stenner said, and glanced at my mother. "I'll be paying the rent."

"When will you and Mommy get married?"

"As soon as I can reach an agreement with Mrs. Stenner."

"When will that be?"

"I don't know. We're negotiating now."

"When will Mommy divorce Daddy?"

"As soon as possible."

"It's all very complicated," my mother said.

I loved the new house and not only because I had two rooms all to myself. The house was located closer to school, which meant I didn't have to spend my entire childhood on a bus. I was going to a private school named Hadley-Coburn, which most of the kids called Hadley-Co, and which some of the kids called Hadley-Co, Inc. You had to wear a uniform at Hadley-Co—plaid skirt, white blouse, blue blazer— and you had to get up at the crack of dawn to catch a bus that took you all over the countryside for six and a half hours picking up *other* kids who went to Hadley-Co. Before we moved into the new house, I used to leave for school at seven-thirty in the morning and get home at a quarter past five, and that was a long hard day.

The new house had a huge lawn that sloped up from the main road to the front door. And it had a pine forest, sort of set back. The pine forest didn't belong to the people who were renting us the house, but that didn't stop me from walking in it. On the ground floor of the house, there was an entrance hall, and then a library to the left of it, and if you walked straight ahead you came into the kitchen and a combination dining room–living room that was connected to the library via a small room that served as a bar. I really *mean* a small room. It probably had been a closet once upon a time, before the owner of the house changed it to a bar by putting in a counter top and a wine rack. Upstairs from the entrance hall, if you went straight ahead, you came to the bedroom I was sleeping in, and a bathroom between *that* bedroom and the one I was spilling over into. Then, if you went down the hall, you came to my mother's bedroom, and across from that the room Mr. Stenner slept in whenever he stayed over.

One of the things I didn't like was Mr. Stenner staying over so often. He came to dinner every single night, and then instead of going home to his own apartment, he usually hung around talking to Mom, and finally she'd say, "Why don't you stay the night, Peter, instead of driving all that distance?"

All that distance was maybe three or four miles. Frankly, I suspected they were sleeping together.

Because otherwise, how come the door at the end of the hall was always locked when Mr. Stenner stayed over, but never locked when there was just Mom and me alone in the house? I was, in fact, positive they were sleeping together. So one morning, I asked my mother if she and Mr. Stenner were sleeping together.

"Yes," my mother said.

"Why?" I said.

"Because we love each other."

"But what about Daddy? Don't you love him?"

"No," my mother said.

"Do you like him?"

"At the moment, no, I don't like him very much either."

"Did you ever like him?"

"Yes, I liked him," my mother said. "And I loved him, too."

"But not anymore."

"No, darling. Not anymore."

"Well . . . *I* love him," I said. "And I like him, too."

"Fine."

"Do you love Mr. Stenner?"

"Yes, Abby. I love him a lot."

"I hate him."

"You told me you liked him. You said you liked him very much."

"That was before he started coming here all the time and acting as if he lived here," I said, and paused, and frowned, and then looked up into my mother's face, and asked the question I should have asked right from the beginning. "Mom," I said, "*does* he live here?"

"Yes," my mother said. "He lives here."

"Shit," I said.

2

I really didn't like him.

First of all, he was always kissing my mother. Every-time I turned around, there he was kissing her. And his breath smelled of tobacco. And on weekends, he didn't shave. And on weekends, he always went around with these ratty sweaters on. One of them had a hole in the sleeve that was eaten by Singapore the cat, who was a Siamese my father had given me on my seventh birthday.

I blamed Mr. Stenner for Singapore getting killed.

I blamed him because he was always mean and rotten to the poor animal, who after all didn't know better than to eat holes in woolen things. Mom asked about it at the pet shop, and also at the veterinarian, and they told her that some Siamese cats did eat wool, they didn't know why, perhaps it was a vitamin deficiency. It was my guess that eating wool was simply Singapore's way. She was, after all, a poor dumb creature. I don't mean stupid, I merely mean dumb. And if you're mean to a creature, the poor thing is going to leave the house and go running down to the dirt road all the time, and sooner or later get hit by an automobile, which was what happened to poor Singapore. Because *he* was mean to her, and only because the poor thing was eating holes in some of his socks and sweaters.

As a matter of fact, Singapore had also eaten a hole in the woolen afghan Grandmother Lu had sent from Palo Alto, California, which was practically my favorite thing in the whole world, but *I* hadn't said a mean word to Singapore about it, had I? No. Because I loved that cat. And Mr. Stenner didn't. And that's why the poor thing got killed. Or at least, that's the way I doped it out. Mr. Stenner came out back with me and helped me dig a little grave under the big elm tree and also made a box to put Singapore in. He even helped me figure out what to say when we buried the cat. But I still didn't like him.

He wasn't like my father.

Before the split, I used to go riding with my father. He used to take me for riding lessons on Saturday mornings at Highland Estates—that was the name of the riding academy. The road that ran past the house we rented after the separation was a dirt road, and Mr. Stenner said that was because a lot of people living on the road kept horses and wanted to ride them around the entire hillside. He said the reason his car had got stuck in the mud the month before was because the people who kept horses always signed petitions every time the town tried to blacktop the road. He was so funny that night his car got stuck in the mud. He came walking up to the house with his pants all dirty and his shoes dripping water, and his hair sticking up, he looked like some kind of monster in a horror movie. And he started ranting and raving about spending an hour and a half on the train from the city, and *then* getting stuck in the mud, people who kept horses should be shot! Mom calmed him down and made a drink for him, and I sat on the couch with my homework spread out on the piano bench in front of me, and stole a look at him, and thought he probably would shoot a horse. In cold blood.

Then one Saturday morning, when I was walking around the hill with him, a man came by riding a horse, and Mr. Stenner watched the horse and rider, and then said, "*God*, that was a beautiful horse, wasn't it?"

"Yeah, but you don't like horses," I said.

"Who says I don't like horses?"

"You said horses should be shot."

"No, I said people who keep horses should be shot."

"That's the same thing," I said.

"It's not," he said. "Let's take in some of these leaves for Mommy, shall we?"

I shrugged.

But I helped him find some pretty leaves for her.

Let me tell you about her conversation with the woman from the telephone company. This was when we first moved into the house Mr. Stenner had rented for us. The house was furnished, and there were phones already in it, but the owner wanted us to contact the phone company to inform them that we were now renting the house, so that we'd be billed for the service each month, instead of him. Mom called the phone company, and asked for the business office, and explained the situation, and figured that was all there'd be to it—from next month on the bills would simply come to Lillith O'Neill on Canterbury Road. But the woman in the business office said, "Have you ever had a telephone before, madam?"

"Yes, certainly," Mom said.

I was sitting on the kitchen floor, playing jacks, and hoping Mr. Stenner wouldn't be coming for dinner as usual. I heard only Mom's side of the conversation, but at the table later she repeated the whole thing to Mr. Stenner, and that's how I learned what the woman in the business office said during the conversation.

"In whose name was your previous telephone listed?" the woman asked.

"My husband's."

"And will this telephone be listed in his name?"

"No," Mom said. "We're separated. We expect to be divorced soon."

"Ah," the woman said. "Then this telephone would be listed in your name, is that correct?"

"Yes."

"I see," the woman said. "Tell me, Mrs. O'Neill, are you at present employed?"

"No," Mom said.

Mom *had* been employed at a literary agency during the first year and a bit more of her marriage, and then she'd got pregnant with me, and from that time on she'd been employed as a wife and mother while Dad climbed the architectural ladder. As she had just told the woman in the business office, however, she was at present unemployed. In fact, she was at present a woman separated from her husband and living in a rented house with her daughter and the man she hoped to marry as soon as a couple of divorces were out of the way. This was a very difficult thing to explain to a woman in the business office of the telephone company. Besides, Mom felt it didn't *have* to be explained.

"Will your husband be paying for this service?" the woman in the business office asked.

"No, he will not," Mom said. "I just told you we're separated." She was beginning to realize where the woman in the business office was going, and she didn't like it. "I've had my own telephone for the past thirteen years," she said. "I certainly . . ."

"Yes, but it was in your husband's name," the woman said. "He was paying the bills."

"So what? *I* was doing the dishes and changing the diapers," Mom said.

"Have you any credit references?" the woman asked.

Had this been last month, or the month before, Mom could have reeled off at least a dozen credit references, because that was how many little plastic cards she'd carried in her wallet. But my father had cut off all her charge privileges the moment she'd told him she was leaving him. She now told the woman in the business office that she did not at present have any credit references.

"I see," the woman said. "In that case, we shall require a sixty-dollar deposit from you. Before we can begin service in your name."

That was when Mom slammed down the telephone receiver with all her might. At dinner that night, Mr. Stenner said, "One of these days the United States is going to declare war on the telephone company."

3

Mr. Stenner was in control in the new house because he was the one paying the rent, and so he was the one telling me to put my napkin on my lap and not do this or that. But my *father* was in control when he picked me up every other weekend after school on Friday, and then brought me back to the house on Canterbury Road after dinner Sunday night. I did not think of that house as home. But I didn't think of my father's house as home, either.

I didn't know where home was.

I knew only that my mother and my father had separated, and that they would never get back together again, and Mom was going to marry Mr. Stenner, who would become my stepfather, and I would have two stepbrothers, who were anyway almost all grown up and wouldn't be any fun. My mother tried to help me with all this. That's why she had all those long serious conversations with me. I remember one conversation —she came into the bedroom and sat on the edge of my bed, and I knew immediately it was going to be a serious conversation. Instead of a bedtime story, she was going to start a serious conversation which I needed like a hole in the head.

"Do you remember the first time you met Mr. Stenner?" my mother asked.

"No, I don't remember," I said.

"You were just a little girl. You were five years old, I think."

"I don't remember."

"Yes, and he came to the house with Mrs. Stenner for drinks one Sunday afternoon. There were quite a few people there, Abby, but you took to Mr. Stenner right away, and singled him out and began talking to him."

"What'd we talk about?"

"Sharks."

"Sharks?"

"Well, not immediately. First you asked each other what your favorite colors were, and your favorite games, and which television shows you liked to watch, and so on. And then you told Mr. Stenner that you hadn't gone in the water at Martha's Vineyard that summer because you were afraid a shark would bite you. You told him you loved to swim, but only in the Koenigs' pool next door, and then you asked him if *he* ever swam in the ocean."

"What did he say?"

"He said yes, he did. And you asked him if he was afraid of sharks, and he said of course he was afraid of sharks, but he liked getting knocked around by the waves, and so he went swimming in the ocean, anyway."

"I don't remember that."

"You asked him what would happen if he ever got bit by a shark, and he said, 'Well, I guess that would be that.' But you were very persistent. You told him he really shouldn't swim in the ocean, and he shouldn't allow Mrs. Stenner to swim in the ocean either, because if a shark ate either one of them then they'd have to get a new wife or husband. That was when you asked him whether he'd get married again if anything ever happened to Mrs. Stenner."

"And what did he say?"

"He said yes, he supposed he'd get married again if anything ever happened to her. And then you asked him *who* he would marry. And he said, 'Who would you like me to marry, Abby?' He was flirting with you, I think. I think he was half-hoping you'd say you wanted him to marry *you*."

"What did I say?"

"You said something very peculiar. You said, 'I'd like you to marry Miss Hayes.'"

"Who's that?"

"Hayes was my maiden name," my mother said.

"I don't remember saying that," I said.

"I think you remember saying it," my mother said.

Maybe I had said it, and wouldn't admit it, or maybe it hadn't been as important to me as it had been to Mom and I'd simply forgotten it. You've got to realize that before the separation Mr. Stenner was just another person who came to the house every now and then. It wasn't until after we all began living together on Canterbury Road that he became such a big deal in my life. So whereas Mom insisted I had said that business about Miss Hayes when I was five years old, I wasn't sure I had. I knew her maiden name was Hayes, of course, because Grandmother Lu was Lucille Hayes, but I doubt very much if I'd have told a perfect stranger (which Mr. Stenner was, after all) that I wanted him to marry my mother, who anyway wasn't Miss Hayes anymore, but who was Mrs. O'Neill, my father's wife.

When I was in kindergarten, there was a little girl whose parents were divorced. The first thing she said to me was, "I'm Karin, my parents are divorced."

"What's that?" I said.

"I don't know," she said, and shrugged.

And in the third grade, there was a little boy who used to cry all the time. I asked him once why he cried so much. He said, "My father lives in a hotel."

I said, "What's so bad about that? I was in a hotel once."

He said, "They've got a separation."

Well, now *I* had a separation, too, and I didn't like it. I wanted my mom and my dad to get back together again. I mean, I was glad Mr. Stenner hadn't turned out to be the kind of man who beats his stepchildren on television or anything like that, but I missed my father, and I wanted Mom to go back to him. As far as I was concerned, "the separation" was responsible for any and all of the ills plaguing my life—like a T-shirt shrinking in the wash, or one of the kids at school calling me a moron. If it weren't for "the separation," there'd be no problems in the entire universe. "The separation" was responsible for everything. If a button fell off my coat, I knew the button would *not* have fallen off if only it weren't for "the separation." It was as simple as that. All the promises of marriage, "once Mr. Stenner and I get our divorces," made no sense at all to me. If they wanted to get divorces, then why didn't they just go out and get them? Instead of hanging around all the time? And hugging and kissing? And doing whatever they were doing behind their closed bedroom door (as if I didn't know).

The last time my mother, my father, and I had been a family together was on Thanksgiving Day, when they'd taken me into the city to see the annual parade. We'd had a good time that day. When we got back home, Mom went into the kitchen to get the turkey going, and Dad and I walked in the woods behind the property. There were leaves all over the ground. Dad and I shuffled through them. He told me that one day he was going to design a house made entirely of leaves. I said, "Dad, you can't build a house of leaves," and he said, "Oh, no? You can't, huh?" and he scooped me up in his arms, and we tumbled to the ground, and rolled around in the leaves, laughing.

Laughing.

It was December now.

I was living on Canterbury Road with Mom and a stranger, and I did not laugh very much these days.

4

The weekends I spent with my father made me happy, and they also made me sad. He would drive up the road to the rented house on top of the hill, and park the car outside the front door, and toot the horn. It was the same car he used to drive when the family was still together. In fact, there was still one of Mom's lipsticks in the glove compartment. He would wait out there in the cold while Mr. Stenner carried my bag downstairs and out to the car.

"Hello, Frank," Mr. Stenner would say.

"Hello, Peter," my father would say. "Ready to go, Abby?"

Mom would come out into the cold, hugging herself, and she would give Dad quick instructions about one thing or another—homework I had to finish, or what time I had to be in bed, or what time she expected me back on Sunday—all clipped and precise. It was very hard for me to imagine that they had ever been married to each other. The truth of the matter, of course, was that they were *still* married to each other. Mom was married to Dad, not Mr. Stenner. Yet it was Dad who came to the house Mr. Stenner was renting, to pick up his own daughter, while Mr. Stenner stood there in the driveway with clouds of vapor coming from his mouth and the trees rattling in the wind. It was somewhat eerie.

Because even though Mom and Mr. Stenner weren't married yet, as I drove away from that big old house every other Friday, I honestly felt as if I were leaving home. As if those two people standing at the top of the driveway watching me leave were really my mother and my father, though I knew that wasn't true. The father part, I mean. Mr. Stenner was *not* my father. He wasn't even my *step*father yet. He was just a man who was living with Mom and me. And helping me with my homework. And telling me not to go charging through the house like a herd of buffalo. And showing me how to do headstands against the wall. And making candles with me from the set Aunt Harriet had sent me for my tenth birthday. And carrying my suitcase to the car, and saying "Hello, Frank" to my father, and then saying "Have a good time, Abby," and standing in the driveway with my mom while the car pulled away.

The house looked warm and cozy up there on top of the hill.

The house I used to live in with my mother and father was smaller than the house we were renting, and my room was downstairs, alongside the laundry room. I have to tell you the truth about this, I didn't like the room I had in my father's house. I'm not sure whether or not I liked that room even when my mother and my father were still living together, but I'm positive I didn't like it when he was living there alone. To begin with, it was downstairs, and I could hear the furnace going, and also I could sometimes hear raccoons prowling around outside the window—*if* they were raccoons. In the dead of night, they sounded like creatures from the black lagoon, and I would lie there with the covers pulled practically to my eyes, listening to the sounds of the monsters outside, and the moaning of the wind didn't help, either, and the creaking of the floorboards, and the furnace going off like a rocket to the moon. Finally, I'd get out of bed and go running barefooted to the steps at the end of the hall, and then go upstairs to my father's bedroom (the one that used to be his and Mom's) and knock on the door, and he'd put on a robe and come out into the living room and we'd talk till I got sleepy enough to go downstairs again.

There wasn't much to talk about. It was very hard to talk to my father. In fact, I did most of the talking. Mr. Stenner was a chatterbox, it was hard to get a word in edgewise when he was around, but my father was a quiet sort of man who never let you know very much about him. I don't remember if we'd had trouble talking to each other before the separation, or if that started afterward, when I was visiting every other weekend. I do know that the conversations we had together were . . . well, uncomfortable.

I remember one weekend—Mom had hired this Norwegian housekeeper, a big husky woman named Berit, and Dad was delayed picking me up. Mom and Mr. Stenner had a dinner date, so they left me with Berit, and Dad came for me later. He was very quiet all through dinner, but I didn't think anything about that because *I* was the one who usually did most of the talking anyway. He was also drinking a lot. I guess maybe the drinking had something to do with what happened when we got back to his house.

He was trying to make a fire, but there was some problem with the flue or the draft or whatever, and he couldn't get it going. It flared up and was fine for a few minutes, and then the flames died down, and the logs began smoking. He put more paper in, and it flared up again and then died again, and I guess he was becoming more and more frustrated. I wasn't even watching him. I was reading a book. I was very interested in the book, as a matter of fact, and I guess he was crying for maybe two or three minutes before I even realized it.

"Dad?" I said.

He didn't say anything, he just kept crying.

"Dad?"

I got up from where I was curled in the leather armchair across the room, and I went to him where he was sitting on the stone floor in front of the fireplace.

He was sitting cross-legged, like an Indian, with his
hands resting on his knees and sort of dangling limply.
Tears were streaming down his face.

"What's the matter?" I said. I was beginning to get
frightened. I'd never seen my father crying before.

"Nothing," he said.

"Then why are you crying?" I said.

"I'm not crying," he said.

"Dad . . ."

"I said I'm not crying!" he shouted.

"Well, then . . ."

"Do you know something?" he said. His eyes were
full of tears, the tears kept brimming over and spilling down his cheeks. He kept gasping for breath as
he talked. "Would you like to know something, Abigail?"

"Yes, Dad," I said, "but please stop crying."

"Your mother is going to divorce me, did you know
that?"

"Yes, Dad."

His nose was running now, he reached for his handkerchief and blew his nose and said again, "Did you
know that, Ab?"

"Yes, Daddy."

"She's not going to be my wife anymore," he said.

"I know."

"She's going to marry that . . ." He blew his nose
again. "Did you know she's going to marry him?"

"Yes, Daddy."

"That son of a *bitch*," he said. "Do you know how
long we've been married, Ab?"

"Thirteen years," I said.

"That's right," he said, sniffing. "How'd you know
that, Ab?"

"Mom told me. Dad, why don't you . . . ?"

"That's a long time to be married to somebody, Ab.
Thirteen years. And now she's just going to get herself
a divorce, she's just going to wipe it all out, just like
that," he said, and tried to snap his fingers, but missed

somehow. "They're going to steal my girl from me," he said.

"No, Dad."

"Yes, they're going to steal my little girl from me," he said, and burst into a torrent of fresh tears. "Do you love me, Ab?" he said.

"I love you, Dad."

He clutched me to him then, and he kept crying into my hair, not saying anything, just crying and crying, and gasping for breath, and holding me very tight.

"Dad," I said, "shall I call Mr. Harkins?" Arthur Harkins was the man who lived across the road. His wife was named Josie Harkins, but she worked for the UN and traveled a lot, and probably wasn't home. "Dad?"

"No," he said. He was still clinging to me, his arms wrapped around me, his tears hot and wet against the side of my neck. And then I got really frightened because in between the tears he just began to ramble, just began saying things that had nothing to do with Mom divorcing him, or at least didn't *seem* to have anything to do with it. Instead, it was as if somebody had opened a pipeline straight into his head. He was talking all this, while crying at the same time, but it sounded instead as if he were thinking it, do you know what I mean?

"*Build* things, that's why," he said. "Put them on paper, see them go up, that's the meaning of it. Two kinds, creators and destroyers, that's all, nobody else, just those. Be different if, sure, but no, not what she wants, oh no. When I told my mother, face lit up, just lit up, architecture, my, my, architecture. Build things. My, my."

"Dad, please let me call Mr. Harkins."

"Couldn't believe it, just couldn't believe it. Come home, nobody here, note on the kitchen table, what kind of way is that? Dear Frank, son of a bitch, dirty rotten son of a bitch . . ."

He shoved me away from him then, shoved me
across the room, and then picked up an ashtray from
the coffee table and threw it against the stone wall of
the fireplace, and I ran out of the room and called
home. Berit answered the phone, and she told me
that my parents weren't back yet. At that time, she
didn't know Mom and Mr. Stenner weren't married;
in fact, she quit the minute she found out. But she'd
heard them mention that they were eating at a restaurant called The Cops and Robbers, and I could
probably get them there if it was important.

"Berit," I said, "there can't be a restaurant called
The Cops and Robbers."

"That's the name," Berit said, and hung up. Berit
spoke English with a heavy accent, and besides was
the kind of woman who thought all children were
nitwits.

In the kitchen, I could hear my father cursing as he
took a tray of ice cubes from the refrigerator, and
tried to get the cubes out of it, and spilled them all
over the floor. I heard the tray when it fell, and heard
the ice skittering over the tiles. I looked up The Cops
and Robbers in the phone book, and couldn't find it,
and then I dialed O for Operator and asked *her* for
The Cops and Robbers, and first she thought I wanted
her to connect me with the police. But when I told
her I was looking for the number of a *restaurant*
called The Cops and Robbers, she told me to dial 411
for Information, which I did, and of course there was
no listing for any such place as The Cops and Robbers. So I looked in Dad's little black book alongside
the telephone, and I called Mr. Harkins after all, but
I didn't want to tell him Dad was out in the kitchen
crying and talking to himself and yelling and what-
not, so I asked him instead if he knew of a restaurant
called The Cops and Robbers, and Mr. Harkins began
laughing, and said, "The *what?*"

"The Cops and Robbers," I said.

"Honeychile," Mr. Harkins said, "there couldn't

possibly be a restaurant called The Cops and Robbers."

"I know," I said.

"You're not thinking of Cobbs Corners, are you?" he asked.

"Maybe," I said. "Thank you, Mr. Harkins."

I hung up, and opened the phone book again, and of course it was Cobbs Corners, however Berit had got The Cops and Robbers from *that* was beyond me. I dialed the number and when somebody answered the phone, I asked to talk to Mrs. Stenner, please. This was the first time I'd ever referred to my mother as that. The person said, "Just a moment, please," and in a minute or so my mother came on the line.

"What's wrong?" she said immediately,

"Daddy's acting funny," I said.

"Funny how?"

"He's swearing and crying and yelling," I said. "Can you come get me, Mommy?"

"We'll be there right away," my mother said.

They picked me up about ten minutes later. My father didn't even come into the driveway to say good-bye. As we drove off, I could see him through the sliding glass doors of the kitchen. He was sitting at the table, staring at his hands, and I suddenly felt I had done the wrong thing by asking my mother to come get me.

When we got home, my mother and Mr. Stenner had a hushed talk in the living room, and I heard Mr. Stenner saying, "I think we'd better call that guy across the road, Lil. What's his name?"

"Arthur Harkins."

"Yeah. Let's call him, okay?"

"Yes," Mom said.

They both went upstairs then, to use the phone in their bedroom. They closed the door behind them, but I could hear Mom's voice anyway. She was talking to Mr. Harkins. She was telling him that Dad seemed to be in pretty bad shape, and would he just go over to make sure everything was all right.

What I couldn't understand was why Mr. Stenner had suggested calling Mr. Harkins. If he *really* cared about what kind of shape my father was in, then he shouldn't have stolen Mom away in the first place.

It was all very confusing.

5

It got particularly confusing around Christmastime.

To begin with, I wasn't sure who was supposed to pay for my father's Christmas present. Because if Mr. Stenner was paying the rent, then he was also paying for our food and clothing, right? And since my mother didn't have any money of her own, then anything she gave me for my father's Christmas present was undoubtedly coming from Mr. Stenner. Which was the same thing as *him* buying a present for my father. Which I'm sure was the last thing in the world he wanted to do, despite the fact that he was the one who'd suggested calling Mr. Harkins that night Daddy got so depressed.

My allowance each week was two dollars—I had no qualms about accepting it from Mr. Stenner, but perhaps that's because I was following Mom's example. I usually spent the money on the following items:

Little glass bottles, which I adored.

Bubble gum, which I similarly adored.

Airmail stamps, to write to Grandmother Lu in California.

I usually got my allowance on Saturday morning. By Saturday afternoon at three o'clock, I had usually *spent* my allowance. So the problem was:

1) How could I buy Daddy a Christmas present with allowances I'd already spent?
2) How could I take money from Mr. Stenner to buy a Christmas present for Daddy?

The way I solved the problem was to cry.

Mr. Stenner came into the living room where I was crying by the fire, and he said, "What's the matter, Abby?"

"You wouldn't understand," I said.

"Don't you want to talk about it?"

"You just wouldn't under*stand*," I said.

"Try me," he said. "Here," he said, and handed me his handkerchief.

I dried my eyes with it, but I didn't blow my nose in it.

"So what's the problem?"

"There's no problem."

"Then why are you crying?"

"Because I *feel* like crying, okay?"

"What about?"

"Nothing."

"If you're crying you must be crying about something."

"It's personal."

"Maybe I can help you with it."

"I doubt it."

"Try me."

"You don't have to keep saying 'Try me, try me,' all the time," I said. "If I feel like trying you, I'll try you."

"Okay, try me," he said, and smiled.

"Boy!" I said, and shot him a piercing look that didn't affect him in the slightest.

"So what is it, Abby?"

"You'd cry, too," I said, "if you didn't have any money of your own, and you had to buy your father a Christmas present, and there was nobody you could ask for money, and you didn't know what to do," I said, and started crying again.

"How about asking me?" Mr. Stenner said.

"Daddy wouldn't want you to pay for his Christmas present."

"Well," Mr. Stenner said, and paused, and then said, "I didn't mean I'd give you the money."

"Huh?" I said, and reached for his handkerchief again.

"Because, frankly, I don't want to pay for your father's present."

"You don't?"

"I don't."

"Well, he doesn't want you to, either."

"I didn't think he'd want me to."

"He doesn't."

"Fine."

"So . . . I still don't know what you mean," I said.

"I could *lend* you the money," Mr. Stenner said. "How much money do you think you'll need?"

"Well, I saw a key chain with his initial on it that cost five dollars and twenty-five cents."

"Five twenty-five, huh?"

"Yes," I said, and nodded. "That's a lot of money."

"I think I can manage it."

"But how would I pay you back?"

"How does ten cents a week sound? There're fifty-two weeks in a year, and if you gave me ten cents a week, you'd have paid back five dollars and twenty cents by the end of a year. How does that sound?"

"It sounds like I'd still owe you a nickel."

"I'd be willing to forget the nickel."

"It also sounds like a very long time," I said.

"It is," he admitted. "What do you say?"

"I think it's a good idea," I said.

"Okay," he said, "it's a deal." He shook hands with me, and then he smiled and said, "But give me back my handkerchief, okay? That's not part of the deal."

So that's how we resolved the matter of Daddy's Christmas present.

It was the night we'd come back from buying the Christmas tree at the empty lot where they were selling them for some benefit, I forget which one. Mr. Stenner left the tree outside in the snow, leaning against the garage wall, and then he came inside blowing on his hands, and asked if anybody would like a fire. My father was always ready to make a fire too, of course, but his weren't as good as Mr. Stenner's. That was because the flue or the draft or whatever was probably better in this house than in my father's. Anyway, we were all sitting around the fire when Mr. Stenner suddenly said, "Lillith, do you have any pictures of yourself when you were pregnant?"

"Why?" my mother said.

"I just wondered what you looked like then."

"I think I have some."

"Could I see them?"

"Well . . . yes. Sure, Peter."

My mother came downstairs a while later with a shoebox full of pictures, and we began looking at them together. There were pictures of me when I was a baby, and pictures of my mother when she was fat as a horse, and pictures of Daddy, too, looking almost like a teen-ager.

And suddenly my mother began crying, and she hugged me to her, and Mr. Stenner just sat there looking stupid and not even realizing he had caused it all, the jackass.

Christmas Day sort of started out to be fun.

My father had given me a tape recorder, and as I opened each of the gifts from my mother and Mr. Stenner, I recorded all of my reactions, so I could play the tape for him later.

"Oh, Daddy!" I shouted into the microphone. "It's a giant Raggedy Ann doll, you should see it! Oh, I *love* it, I *love* it, just a minute, Daddy," and I clicked off the machine until I'd unwrapped another gift, and then *click* went the little button again, and I shrieked, "Daddy, it's a *hair* dryer! It's all pink, and it has a comb and a brush and a spot concentrator, wait till you *see* it, Daddy!"

Then, after all the gifts had been opened and the

wrappings burned in the fireplace, I asked Mr. Stenner to listen while I played back the tape.

"Thanks, I heard it the first time around," Mr. Stenner said, and went out into the kitchen.

I followed him and said, "But you didn't hear the *tape*. Will you listen to the tape with me?"

"I'll listen to part of the tape."

"Why can't you listen to all of it?"

"Because the boys'll be here any minute."

"If we have time to play all of it before the boys come . . ."

"No, I don't want to hear all of it," Mr. Stenner said.

"Why not?"

"Abby, just play some of it, okay?"

"Well, okay," I said, and shrugged, and put on the tape.

The boys arrived at a little past noon.

My mother had told me that when she and Mr. Stenner finally got married, the boys would be my stepbrothers. I wasn't too sure whether I liked that idea. I didn't think my mother liked it much, either. Whenever the boys were around, she got very quiet. Jeff was the oldest of Mr. Stenner's sons, and he didn't look like Mr. Stenner at all. My mother had told me that Jeff resembled Mrs. Stenner, but I could hardly remember what Mrs. Stenner looked like. All I knew was that Jeff had sort of reddish hair, and a beard that was part red and part gold, whereas Mr. Stenner's hair was brown and he didn't have a beard at all. So I guessed maybe Jeff *did* resemble Mrs. Stenner instead of his father. Not that Mrs. Stenner had a beard.

The second son was named Luke. He never looked into Mommy's eyes. It was almost as if by not *looking* at her, he would not be *seeing* her. I knew exactly how he felt. Lots of times, I'd close my *own* eyes and wish that Mr. Stenner would be gone when I opened them. It never worked. In the kitchen, while Mommy was fixing the salad, Luke suddenly asked, "How old are you, anyway, Lillith?"

Mommy turned from the counter top and looked into his face. "I'm thirty-six," she said.

"Pop's forty-three," Luke said.

I knew what he was thinking. Mr. Stenner was too *old* for Mommy, that's what he was thinking. Daddy was just the right age, thirty-eight.

I decided I was going to like Luke.

The Christmas tree was hung with neckties.

The ties belonged to my father. I'd been to visit him the weekend before and had come home with a dozen or more of his old ties, which I'd knotted together, end to end, and wound around the small tree in the living room.

"How does it look?" I asked Jeff, the oldest son.

Jeff stepped back from the tree, put his hands on his hips, and cocked his head to one side. "Let's say it's an unusual tree," he said.

"Those are her father's ties," Mr. Stenner said.

"First tree I've ever seen with neckties on it," Jeff said.

"Might set a trend," Mr. Stenner said, and smiled.

"What's so funny?" I asked. "There's nothing funny about ties."

They were talking about the house. They were all sitting in the living room after Christmas dinner, and Mr. Stenner was putting another big log onto the fire, and my mother was saying how lucky we'd been to find a house like this on such short notice. My mother was looking into the fire, and didn't see the glance Luke directed at her. I saw it, though, and knew at once what it meant. In Luke's eyes, our finding a place to stay hadn't been good fortune at all. Luke would have considered *all* of us luckier if we'd stayed where we belonged—Mommy and me in *our* house with

Daddy, and Mr. Stenner *home* with his wife and sons. Never mind *this*. What was *this* supposed to be, anyway? They weren't even married, who were they trying to kid here?

"Well, it's not a bad house," Mr. Stenner said, and poked at the fire, and then stood up and closed the fireplace screen. "Trouble is, it comes complete with the Mauley curse."

"What's that?" Jeff asked, and laughed.

"Mr. Mauley, our landlord. See that painting on the wall? The man wearing the British cavalry officer's uniform? That's one of his ancestors."

"Speaking of ancestors," Jeff said, "I wish Grandma and Grandpa could've made it today."

"They're not ancestors yet," Luke said.

"I'm sorry they aren't here," Jeff said. "I miss them."

"Well, they went down to Florida early this year," Mr. Stenner said.

"Mm," Jeff said.

"I think they felt a bit uncomfortable about coming here today," Mr. Stenner said.

"Gee, I wonder why," Luke said suddenly.

"What does that mean, Luke?" Mr. Stenner asked.

"Well, it is a pretty unusual arrangement, Pop."

"Really? I thought kids today were used to all sorts of arrangements."

"Just one difference, Pop," Luke said.

"Yeah, and what's that?"

"*You're* not a kid."

It was Jeff, though, who started the hassle later that night. Aunt Harriet had called from New Mexico, and I'd gone to the phone to talk to her, and I overheard the beginning of the conversation while I was thanking Aunt Harriet for the silver and turquoise bracelet and ring. Jeff had asked his father why he'd stopped sending Mrs. Stenner money, and Mr. Stenner said he had not stopped sending her money, he had simply stopped sending her as much money. Jeff wanted to know why he'd done that, did he want her to starve? Mr. Stenner very calmly answered that Jeff's mother was not about to starve, and that he was only following his lawyer's advice in reducing the monthly payments to her, a move designed to get her to negotiate again.

"If you're so hot to negotiate," Jeff said, his voice rising, "why the hell don't you talk to her personally, instead of through the goddamn lawyers?"

In the kitchen, I suddenly began trembling.

"I have nothing to say to her personally," Mr. Stenner said.

"Do you realize you're the only one who wants this divorce?" Jeff said. "Mom doesn't want it, I don't want it, Luke doesn't want it . . ."

"That's right," Mr. Stenner said. "*I* want it."

"That's pretty selfish, isn't it, Pop?" Luke asked.

"Yes, it's selfish," Mr. Stenner said.

"She still loves you, do you realize that?"

"Luke . . ."

"No matter what you've done, she still loves you," Jeff said.

In the kitchen, I held my breath, waiting for Mr. Stenner's answer.

"I don't love her," he said softly.

"Well," Luke said, and sighed.

"Well, the hell with it," Jeff said. "Let's go home, Luke."

After they left I saw Mr. Stenner sitting alone in the living room, staring at the flames in the fireplace. Once, he glanced up at the painting of the British cavalry officer on the wall.

Then he looked back at the fire again.

6

In January, a lot of trouble started.

First of all, my father went to France for two weeks to talk to a company about designing a big industrial complex for them in Marseilles, wherever *that* was. I missed him dreadfully, even though he sent a post-card each and every day of the week, including Sundays. But I knew what hotel he was staying at in Marseilles, and I also knew the time difference, because I'd asked Mrs. Jovet, who taught French at Hadley-Co. So one fine Friday night, when Mom and Mr. Stenner went to a movie and left me with a sitter, I picked up the telephone and made a collect, trans-atlantic, person-to-person call to Mr. Frank O'Neill at the Grand Hotel et Noailles in Marseilles. It was eight o'clock at night when I made the call, but like magic it became two o'clock in the morning when Dad picked up the phone. He sounded very sleepy and fuzzy at first, but then we had a nice long chat. I told him I missed him and wished he would hurry back home, and then we said good night to each other, though for him it was already morning, and I went downstairs to tell the sitter I was going to bed.

In the morning, at the breakfast table, I mentioned that I had called Dad in Marseilles.

"You *what?*" Mom said.

"Don't worry," I said. "I reversed the charges."

"Who gave you permission to call Marseilles?" my mother asked.

"I didn't know I needed permission," I said. "You

said I could call Dad whenever I wanted, didn't you?"

"Yes, but . . ."

"Well, I felt like calling him, so I called him."

"What was so urgent that you had to call all the way to . . . ?"

"Nothing was urgent. You said I could call him whenever I wanted to, so I called him. Isn't that what she said, Mr. Stenner? That I could call Dad whenever . . ."

"Yes, that's what she said."

"See? So I felt like calling, so I . . ."

"*But,*" Mr. Stenner said.

I looked at him.

"You're taking advantage of a technicality," he said.

"What does that mean?" I said.

"It means you know very well what we meant when we . . ."

"We? Who's *we?* It was Mom who made the decision about the phone calls."

"No, it was Mom and I together."

"It was Mom who told me I could call Dad whenever . . ."

"Yes, it was Mom who told you. But it was Mom and I who . . ."

"What'd *you* have to do with it?"

"Mom and I make all the decisions together around here."

"Even decisions about my father?"

"Yes, even decisions about your father."

"I don't see why you should have anything to say about calls *I* make to *my* father. If I want to call my own father . . ."

"Abby," Mr. Stenner said, "we're not going to get into a contest with your father. We told you it was okay to call him whenever you wanted, but I think you know that didn't mean calling him in France."

"You're not to do that again," my mother said.

"Well, where can I call him? Can I call him in Germany or Spain or . . . ?"

"Is he going to Germany or Spain?" Mr. Stenner asked.

"I don't know where he's going. I'm just saying . . ."

"Then don't worry about it."

"I'm trying to find out what's okay and what isn't okay around here. I make a lousy call to France—that you didn't even have to *pay* for—and next thing I know . . ."

"Abby," Mr. Stenner said, "it is *not* okay to make any long-distance calls without first asking our permission. Does that clarify it for you?"

"What's considered long distance? Is it long distance to call . . ."

"You know what long distance is."

"No, I don't."

"Then pick up the phone and ask the operator what the local dialing distance is. Anything outside of that is long distance."

"I don't know how to do that," I said.

"You knew how to call Marseilles," Mr. Stenner said, and put his napkin on the table, and got up, and went out into the living room.

The Rules List went up the next morning.

I think I already mentioned that when you came into the house the first thing you saw was a staircase going up to where the bedrooms were. The side of the staircase formed a passageway that led to the kitchen, and was paneled with wood. Mr. Stenner had decorated the wood paneling with black-and-white enlargements of pictures he had taken, though he was afraid Mr. Mauley would come in one day and tell him to take the pictures down.

Mr. Mauley had come around on New Year's Day to wish us a happy new year, and while he was in the house, he'd gone up to my room to check on a storm window that was flapping. He'd noticed that Mr. Stenner had put up a mobile I'd made, and he started fussing and fretting about making holes in the ceiling, and about how difficult it was to repair ceilings when tenants put holes in them. Mr. Stenner very slowly and precisely told Mr. Mauley that the mobile was made of string and cardboard and was light enough to be held to the ceiling with a simple straight pin. Mr. Stenner had, in fact, very carefully and gently hammered the straight pin into the ceiling for me, being careful not to damage anything up there—as if a straight pin *could* damage anything. He had in fact bent fourteen pins before he got one to go in right.

Mr. Mauley hemmed and hawed and harrumphed a lot, but I think he got Mr. Stenner's message about not bugging us over a simple little pinhole in the ceiling. But Mr. Stenner *was* worried now about the photographs he'd put up on the side of the staircase. Anyway, that's where the Rules List was. Mr. Stenner had taken down one of the photographs, the one I loved of the swan, and had put the Rules List up in its place. The list was hand-lettered. He was pretty good at stuff like that, though not as good as Dad. This is what it looked like:

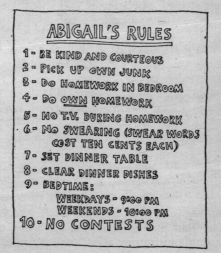

ABIGAIL'S RULES

1 - BE KIND AND COURTEOUS
2 - PICK UP OWN JUNK
3 - DO HOMEWORK IN BEDROOM
4 - DO OWN HOMEWORK
5 - NO T.V. DURING HOMEWORK
6 - NO SWEARING (SWEAR WORDS COST TEN CENTS EACH)
7 - SET DINNER TABLE
8 - CLEAR DINNER DISHES
9 - BEDTIME:
    WEEKDAYS - 9:00 PM
    WEEKENDS - 10:00 PM
10 - NO CONTESTS

They called me down for breakfast, and the very first thing I saw on the way to the kitchen was the list. I read it silently, and then I went into the kitchen. Mr. Stenner was at the stove, making pancakes. Mr. Stenner considered pancakes quote a family tradition unquote. All he knew how to cook was pancakes. My father could cook sea bass and quiche and all sorts of things. In fact, before the split, one of the few times my parents didn't argue was when they were planning and cooking a meal together. Mr. Stenner made pancakes every Sunday morning. That's because he used to make pancakes for his sons every Sunday morning. The one thing he didn't realize was that his sons really *were* his family whereas I was *not* his family. Mom wasn't either. So the quote family tradition unquote was wasted on us. Or at least on me.

They were playing it cool, both of them. They knew I'd seen the list, knew I'd read it, and were waiting for me to make the first comment. I didn't disappoint them.

"What do you mean swear words cost ten cents each?" I asked.

"If you swear," Mr. Stenner said, "we'll deduct ten cents from your allowance for each . . ."

"Why?"

"Because it isn't nice for little girls to use the kind of language you've been using," Mom said.

"Language like what?"

"You know what," Mr. Stenner said.

"Give me an example of the words I can't use," I said.

Mr. Stenner looked me straight in the eye and said, "Shit."

"Okay," I said, and shrugged.

"And I think you know the other words," he said.

"Can I say them now, just to make sure we're both thinking of the same words? I mean, will it cost me a dime if I say them now?"

"Yes."

"Then how can I be sure . . ."

"You can be sure we're both thinking of the same words," Mr. Stenner said.

"It didn't cost *you* anything," I said. "When you said . . ."

"Careful," he said.

"Can I spell it?"

"No."

"Well, it didn't cost you anything."

"When you get to be forty-three years old, you can say whatever you want, too. Meanwhile, it'll cost you a dime."

"That isn't fair."

"Who says it has to be fair?"

"Huh?"

"Nowhere is it written that grown-ups have to be fair to children," he said, and flipped a pancake.

"Boy!" I said.

"Right," he said, and flipped another pancake. He was smiling, the rat.

"And what's this about doing my own homework? I *do* do my own homework."

"Mommy and I do it," he said.

"You mean because I ask a simple question every now and then?"

"Always."

"Only every now and then."

"*Always.* There are three things going on every time you do your homework, Abby. The first thing is the television set . . ."

"I don't even *watch* it. I just like to hear the voices. Television helps me concentrate."

Mr. Stenner rolled his eyes.

"It does."

"No television," he said.

"Okay, no damn television."

"And that's ten cents," he said.

"Shit," I said.

"And that's another . . ."

"All right, all *right!*" I said.

"And no doing your homework in the living room. That's the second thing that's going on, all the chatter between Mommy and me, which you're just dying to hear. You've got the television on, and you're listening to our conversation . . ."

"What's the third thing?"

"The third thing is constantly asking us what a word means, or how to do an arithmetic problem, or where India is . . ."

"I *know* where India is."

"I think you understand what we're trying to tell you, Abby," my mother said.

"All right, I'll turn off the television, all right? But I'll do my homework down here."

"No, you'll do it upstairs in your bedroom. There's a desk in your bedroom, that's what desks are for."

"I like to spread out."

"No, you just like to be in the middle of things," my mother said.

"There's too much happening down here," Mr. Stenner said. "You can't possibly concentrate on what you're supposed to be doing when . . ."

"I promise I won't ask any more questions while I'm doing my homework, okay?"

"No," Mr. Stenner said.

"Well, why not? If I turn off the television, and I keep quiet . . ."

"*We* want some time alone," Mr. Stenner said.

"What?"

"I said . . ."

"I heard what you said. You're alone every night after I go to bed, what do you mean you . . ."

"When I get home from work," Mr. Stenner said, "there are lots of things I want to discuss with Mom, most of them private. If you're sitting here in the living room, with your books sprawled all over the floor . . ."

"Well, if you've got something private to tell her, why don't you go upstairs, instead of me?"

"Because you're the poor, put-upon little kid," Mr. Stenner said, smiling, "and I'm your mean old stepfather."

"You're not my stepfather yet, thank God."

"I will be soon."

"You know what I'm going to do? I'm going to save all my homework and do it at Daddy's when I go to see him. Because when I ask *him* questions, he always . . ."

"That's rule number ten," Mr. Stenner said.

"Huh?"

"No contests," he said. "Would you like another pancake?"

"No," I said. "I *hate* pancakes."

Two days before the end of January, they left me with a woman named Mrs. Cavallo while they went down to Haiti for Mom's divorce. They were only gone overnight, but I must've called Dad at least a dozen times while they were gone. Mrs. Cavallo didn't know what was going on. They had told her about the Rules List, and showed her where it was tacked up to the side of the staircase, but I took the list down the minute they drove off, and when Mrs. Cavallo looked for it I told her the wind probably blew it off the wall while the door was open and they were carrying their bags out. Miraculously, the wind blew it back onto the wall, pushpins and all, just before they got home the next day. Mrs. Cavallo told them I'd been a good girl while they were gone, and she also told them I'd spent a lot of time on the telephone with my father.

"You're not her father?" she asked Mr. Stenner, smiling.

"No," Mr. Stenner said.

"Ah," Mrs. Cavallo said, and clucked her tongue. "A second marriage, eh?"

"Yes," my mother said.

"Ah," Mrs. Cavallo said again, and counted the money twice when Mr. Stenner paid her for her services.

At dinner that night, Mom told me about Haiti, about how hot it had been down there, and about the beggars on the courthouse steps and on the columned verandah facing a public pump from which a pregnant woman kept drawing water. The woman had made six trips to the pump before Mom was called into the judge's presence, back and forth over the rock-strewn road, her enormous belly thrust out ahead of her, the laden buckets at the ends of her arms serving almost as counterweights to the unborn child inside her. And then Mom had gone into the courthouse while Mr. Stenner waited outside, and the Miami lawyer representing her had secured the divorce in exactly four minutes. That was how long it had taken. Mom was still amazed that all it had taken was four minutes. Signed, sealed, and delivered —*sealed* yes. There was a great blob of red sealing wax on the divorce decree, over a pair of flowing red ribbons.

"Why'd *you* go with her?" I asked Mr. Stenner.

"What do you mean?" he said.

"If Mommy went down there to divorce Daddy, why didn't *he* go with her? He was the one who married her in the first place, wasn't he? So he should have been the one to go get the divorce with her."

My mother's wineglass hesitated on the way to her lips. She told me later that she'd thought the exact same thing coming home on the plane, and had suddenly buried her head in Mr. Stenner's shoulder and begun crying. She hadn't told him why she was crying. She hadn't said she considered it somehow barbaric to divorce a man without him being there to hear those final words spoken—the way he'd heard the marriage words spoken before an assemblage of witnesses more than thirteen years before.

The wineglass hesitated on the way to her lips, and Mom sipped at the wine thoughtfully, and then turned to me and said, "Daddy signed a power of attorney. He didn't have to be there."

"Neither did Mr. Stenner," I said flatly.

7

Whenever a kid from school was visiting, I used to introduce Mr. Stenner as my stepfather, even though he wasn't yet. I think I was embarrassed about Mom and him living together without being married.

I'd say, "This is my stepfather," and they'd say, "Hi." Simple as that.

But not so simple.

I didn't *want* him to be my stepfather.

I used to take my mother aside and casually say, "Are you really going to marry him?"

"Yes," she would say. She was having a lot of trouble right then with a lawyer named Arthur Randolph Knowles, who was Mr. Stenner's attorney. He had, in fact, been Mr. Stenner's attorney for years, and had insisted that his firm handle the divorce, even though there were no divorce specialists in his office. At least, that's what Mom said. The only time she and Mr. Stenner came close to having an argument, in fact, was when they were discussing Arthur Randolph Knowles.

It seemed to me, though, that he wanted exactly the same thing I wanted. He wanted Mr. Stenner to go back to his wife and children, and the hell with Mommy and me. But even if there was nothing I'd have liked better than for Mr. Stenner to have shaken hands with Mom and sailed off into the sunset, I still didn't like Arthur Randolph Knowles. He was a pompous little man who always stood in front of the fireplace with his hands on his little potbelly, toasting his backside. Every time he opened his mouth, I expected dusty butterflies to come out. He always talked about the divorce in front of me, probably because he was one of those people who thought children didn't exist. This is what he sounded like:

"As you know, Peter, the present status of your marital problem is that you have reduced Joan's support payments, and have cut off all her charge accounts, credit cards, et cetera, et cetera."

"Et cetera, et cetera" is precisely what Arthur Randolph Knowles used to say. Joan, by the way, was Mr. Stenner's wife. Whenever they talked about her, I tried to remember what she looked like. I recalled a blue-eyed woman with dark brown hair. Once, when I was visiting Dad on a weekend, he pointed a woman out to me and said, "There's Mrs. Stenner," but she was getting into an automobile, and I didn't get a good look at her.

"I am sure," Mr. Knowles said, "that Joan must be bitterly unhappy with the present arrangement, which is so financially favorable to you, Peter, and so the next move is up to her and her lawyer."

"Arthur," Mr. Stenner said, "all I want to know is what options are open to us, that's all. That's why I asked you to come here tonight. Lillith and I . . ."

"Yes, I quite understand."

"That's what we'd like to know."

"Yes. I'm coming to that, Peter. Patience, m'boy."

Every time he said "Patience, m'boy," Mom winced.

"Because it's been almost seven months now, and there's no sign . . ."

"What would you like, Peter? Would you like *Joan* to sue for divorce? I assure you there are grounds freely available to her," Mr. Knowles said, and began ticking off the grounds on his fingers. "Abandonment, infidelity, failure to provide adequately for her support, et cetera, et cetera. But do you really want her to sue for divorce?"

"Arthur, you're the lawyer, why are you asking me for advice?" Mr. Stenner said.

"The question was rhetorical," Mr. Knowles said, "and the answer is 'Of course not!' Were she to sue for divorce, she would make immediate application for temporary alimony and counsel fees in substantial amounts. Moreover, were she even to sue for a legal separation . . ."

He went on and on, lawyers really *are* full of it. The gist of what he said each and every time was that without the cooperation of Mr. Stenner's wife, it was of course enormously difficult to obtain an equitable separation agreement. Mrs. Stenner did not want a divorce. Therefore . . .

Arthur Randolph Knowles shrugged, and smiled, and looked at my mother. The smile seemed to be advising her to forget the entire matter, let the man go back to his wife and children, eh? Then Mr. Knowles turned to Mr. Stenner and said, "As I've told you many times, Peter, marital problems of this sort can be most time-consuming, but in the long run, we always find a way to work them out, one way or the other. I strongly counsel your patience and forbearance. This too shall pass."

Later that night, after Mr. Knowles had left, Mom said, "I despise the way that man expresses himself. Why does he always use language that sounds so medieval?"

"Bitterly unhappy," Mr. Stenner quoted.

"Patience and forbearance."

"This too shall pass."

There was more snow in February and March than I could remember seeing ever in my life. Snow meant clogged roads. Clogged roads meant Dad having trouble picking me up on weekends. I was always waiting for something, it seemed. Waiting for Dad to come get me, or waiting for the divorce, or the wedding, or something, I don't know what. Something terribly dramatic, I guess. A knock at the door. A lightning bolt zigzagging through the window and hitting the portrait of the cavalry officer. Anything. In the meantime, the three of us moved through that house like actors who'd already spoken our lines and gone to where we were supposed to go onstage, and were—well, waiting.

Just waiting.

I didn't want Mr. Stenner to get his divorce, I didn't want him and Mom to get married, and yet I did. I hated him, you see. But I also liked him a lot. He was a very comical man. And noisy. God, was he noisy. Once he had to go to Philadelphia to take some pictures there for a magazine, and he was gone only overnight, but I remember going into the living room where Mom was reading and saying to her, "Boy, it's quiet around here."

He was always making noise, if you know what I mean.

If a song he liked started playing on the radio, he'd just sing along with it at the top of his lungs. He had the world's worst voice, he sang off key. I'd say, "That's not the way it goes, Mr. Stenner," and he'd say, "Quiet, Abby, that's the way it goes." And I'd try to teach him the right tune and he'd listen and then try to repeat it and get it all wrong again, a true tin ear, worse than Mom's, which was also pretty tinny. Or he'd start dancing in what he considered rock style, shaking his fanny around the living room and wagging his hands in the air. A song would come on, and he'd just jump up off the couch and start dancing to beat the band! He wasn't showing off or anything, he'd do it even if he was alone in the room, you'd suddenly feel the walls shaking, you knew Mr. Stenner was in there dancing all by himself, shaking his behind and wagging his hands.

At the dinner table, he'd talk all the time. You could hardly get a word in edgewise. He'd tell you all about his day—a model *bit* him one day, right on the second joint of his index finger! He came home with the finger in a bandage, and he told us all about this crazy model who, because he was pointing to a spot he wanted her to focus her gaze on, bit him on the finger! He showed me her picture in a magazine, she looked so sweet butter wouldn't melt. But she'd bit his finger almost clear to the bone. He told Mom he would have crowned her with his camera except that it was such an expensive instrument and he was afraid it would smash to pieces on her hard head.

He had a great sense of outrage and indignation. I really liked that about him, too. Remember I told you about the horses, about the road being a quagmire because people kept horses and wouldn't allow other people to get it paved? Well, that was an example of the kind of thing that infuriated him and of course started him yelling around the house. People being oblivious to other people's needs. If, for example, we were picking up something at the tailor shop and a lady just came through the door, barging into us without apologizing, practically without even *see*-ing us, Mr. Stenner would roll his eyes and say, "Oh, Blivious!" Meaning "oblivious." Meaning the lady was oblivious to anyone but herself. He also had a way of breaking words in half so that it sounded as if he were using a person's name.

He would, for example, say, "What's the troub, Bill?"

Or, "Pass the sher, Bert."

Or, "They buried him in the semmer, Terry."

Or, "I'm the host, Tess."

Or he'd come over to me—this was a different word game—and he'd say, "Hi, Abby. Jeet?" And I was supposed to answer, "No, joo?" and he would then say, "Squeet." Jeet, joo, squeet—which translated into:

"Did you eat?"

"Did you?"

"Let's go eat."

Jeet, joo, squeet.

He told me some peachy stories. He used to make them up as he went along, and most of them were about me though he tried to disguise them by saying they were about a whale in the ocean or a star in the sky, or whatever. One night, he really broke me up. I was begging him to tell me a story, and he was telling me it was already a quarter to ten, fifteen minutes past my bedtime (we were pretty much living by the Rules List, and I'll tell you the truth, it wasn't so bad), but I kept begging, and finally he said, "Okay, but it'll be a very short story."

"Okay," I said.

"Okay," he said. "Once upon a time, there was this very short bear." Then he leaned over the bed and kissed me on the cheek and said, "Good night, Abby, sleep well."

"Hey!" I said. "That isn't fair."

But I was smiling.

Spring was here!

Mr. Stenner was going out to take pictures of things budding!

And he had a camera for me to use!

It was one of his old cameras, but in perfectly good condition, and not a baby camera at all. You had to load the film yourself, and you had to focus, and set the exposure, and the speed—it was a pretty complicated instrument to handle but Mr. Stenner was very patient, and never once lost his temper even when I was fussing about with all those dials and gadgets.

With my camera around my neck like Mr. Stenner, I waved to Mom, and both of us went tramping off into the woods in search of budding things.

He had a great eye.

He could spot something two miles away, I mean it.

"Shhhh," he'd say, as if the plant were a living thing that could hear us and go scurrying off into the bushes. Then we would tiptoe through the woods, and he would motion for me to be very still, and he would part some leaves, and there it was, a sweet white violet, or a beautiful red columbine or yellow lady's slipper. He knew the name of every wild flower in the woods, he was absolutely fantastic when it came to reeling them off. They sounded like poetry. Yellow clintonia and star grass and trailing arbutus and Dutchman's-breeches (*that* one made me laugh), and wild sarsaparilla and false spikenard and Pipsissewa and Queen Anne's lace—oh, God, we had such fun that day!

He was, you know, alive.

When we had Field Day at Hadley-Co, I was on red team, and I asked Mr. Stenner to come to school with Mom that afternoon. I also asked him to bring his camera. At Hadley-Co, the most important clique was led by a girl named Sarah Prentiss, and I'd tried to make friends with her by telling her my stepfather was a famous fashion photographer. He wasn't exactly famous, but he *was* a professional photographer and he did photograph famous models like the one who'd almost bit off his finger. Sarah said she wanted to see some of the pictures he'd taken, and I went home and asked Mr. Stenner for some magazines and brought them in with me the next day. Sarah looked at the magazines. Then, surrounded by all her friends in the clique, she said, "Even *I* can take better pictures than *that.*"

So at Field Day, I introduced Sarah to Mr. Stenner.

"This is my stepfather," I said. "This is Sarah Prentiss."

"Hi," Sarah said.

"Hi," Mr. Stenner said.

"And this is my mother."

"Hi."

"Sarah says she can take better pictures than you," I said.

Sarah blinked.

"She probably can," Mr. Stenner said, and smiled. "Why don't both of you stand there like silly grinning little girls and I'll take a picture of you together?"

"Okay," Sarah said.

He took a picture of us looking like silly grinning little girls. It came out very nice, as a matter of fact, and he had a print blown up for Sarah, who later said it was probably only the best picture anybody ever took of her, and who also mentioned that it was taken by Peter Stenner, the famous fashion photographer.

Red team lost every event, and also the tug-of-war.

I ate four hot dogs.

Mr. Stenner took three rolls of pictures, thirty-six pictures on each roll. In color.

Every time I looked around, there he was with the camera to his eye.

I couldn't wait to show the pictures to Daddy.

At a Tuesday meeting in the merry, merry month of May, much to Arthur Randolph Knowles's "utter astonishment," Mrs. Stenner's lawyer proposed satisfactory settlement terms, and Mr. Knowles immediately called Mr. Stenner to recommend acceptance. The case of *Stenner v. Stenner* seemed resolved at last, and a jubilant Mr. Knowles called again later in the afternoon to say that the separation agreement would be drawn at once. As soon as the papers were signed, Mr. Stenner would be free to fly to Haiti or the Dominican Republic for a divorce similar to the quickie Mom had got in January.

At the dinner table that night, Mr. Stenner did an imitation of Mr. Knowles saying, "I *told* you it would take a little patience, didn't I, m'boy?"

"I'm glad it's resolved," Mom said, in what was perhaps the understatement of the year.

8

Did I tell you about the bronze cats?

I guess not.

It's funny how things that are really important can slip your mind.

Mr. Stenner tried so hard to make pancakes a tradition with us, but failed. Instead, without his having to try so very hard at all, the bronze cats did become a tradition. He gave me the first one on Christmas Day—the day Dad gave me the tape recorder and I was opening all my gifts and telling Dad what they were, which I now realize was a very cruel thing to do. I did what may seem like a cruel thing on their wedding day, too, but maybe if you understand what was going on in my head you won't think it was so cruel. Anyway, the only person I was really cruel to was myself. *Both* days.

On Christmas Day, I was cruel to myself because I was trying so hard to make sure Daddy shared everything that I almost missed what was happening. I mean, how can you really enjoy opening presents when you've got to give a blow-by-blow report to a tape recorder because you're afraid your father is all alone in a big empty house weeping by the fire. Which he wasn't. Actually, he spent Christmas Day with his brother in Mamaroneck. The one thing I didn't describe to the tape recorder was the bronze cat Mr. Stenner gave me.

The box was marked "To Abby from Mr. Stenner." It was a small box, maybe two inches square and an inch high, but whatever was in it weighed a ton! What was in it was a gray-striped tabby lying on his back on two puffy blue pillows, and playing with a red ball. The pillows were enameled bronze, same as the cat, but they looked so soft it was almost impossible to believe they were made of metal. I opened the box and was reaching for the RECORD button on the machine when I suddenly realized I shouldn't be telling Dad about something Mr. Stenner had given me, because this might get Dad angry or depressed. Or maybe I just felt this was something private, between me and Mr. Stenner—something Dad shouldn't share. I really don't know.

But in that second when I saw the little striped pussycat holding the red ball between his front paws and sinking into those stuffed pillows, I thought of Singapore the cat who'd got run over, and I thought about Mr. Stenner helping me to bury Singapore out back, and about him helping me with the right words to say at the funeral. And I thought it was very kind and sensitive of him to buy me a miniature bronze cat for Christmas, something special from him to me, even though I had no idea at the time that we were starting a tradition.

That was the first of the cats.

I got the second cat on the day they were married.

Early that morning, Mom came into my bedroom wearing her serious face, so I knew we were going to have a meaningful talk. She sat on the edge of my bed, took my right hand between both her hands, and said, "Well, Abby, here we are."

"Mm," I said.

"How do you feel?" Mom said.

I shrugged.

"Are you happy?" Mom asked.

"Oh, Mom," I said, "do you have to marry him?" and threw myself into her arms like a three-year-old and began weeping. "I don't *want* you to marry him," I said. "I don't want him to be my stepfather, I want us to go back to Daddy, I want to live with Daddy, I want both of us to live with Daddy, I don't like Mr. Stenner, I hate Mr. Stenner, please don't marry him, Mom, I'll do anything you ask in my entire lifetime, I swear to God, if you just won't marry him, just do me that one favor."

"No," Mom said.

"Mom, please, I'll throw myself out the window if you marry him, I'll throw myself in front of a car, I'll . . ."

"You'll do no such thing," Mom said.

"Mom, can't you see it'll make me miserable? Can't you see I'll hate him as long as I live, I'll . . . ?"

"That would be a terrible shame," Mom said. "He's a good man, Abby. You'd be missing a lot by hating him instead of loving him."

"Shit, I love *Daddy!*" I shouted.

Mom didn't say anything to that. She didn't even fine me ten cents. She just kept hugging me close and patting my shoulder and whispering things against my hair. Just before she left the room she said, "Will you be all right, darling?"

I nodded.

"Bless your heart," she said, and went out.

When Mr. Stenner came in about ten minutes later, I was still crying. Mom always told him everything, but I could tell she hadn't told him about the conversation we'd just had. He seemed honestly surprised to find me crying.

"Hey," he said. "What's the prob, Lum?"

"Nothing," I said.

"Need a handkerchief?"

"No."

"Why the tears?"

"None of your business," I said.

"Okay," he said. "Here's something for you."

"What is it?" I said, and sniffed.

"Little present," he said, and handed me a small box wrapped with white paper and tied with a pink ribbon. "Commemorate this happy occasion," he said, and then said, "Sob, sob."

"Don't make fun of me," I said.

"Who's making fun of you? Those *are* tears of joy, aren't they?"

I shot him an angry look, and then loosened the ribbon, and tore the wrapping paper off the box, and lifted first the lid and then the square of cotton that was lying on top of the present. The present, of course, was another bronze cat. A striped tabby. Two inches tall. Standing on his hind legs. His tail trailing behind him on the floor. In his left paw, he was holding a bright red rose against his chest.

"That's because you'll be handing out the flowers," Mr. Stenner said.

"I know," I said. "Thank you."

"You're welcome," he said.

The day could not have been more perfect.

The wedding and reception were to take place in Arthur Randolph Knowles's eighteenth-century house, and he kept telling the assembled guests that he had ordered the day months in advance just to be absolutely certain of cloudless blue skies and balmy breezes. "One can't be too careful when making requests of the Supreme Being, now can one?" he said, and I still thought he was an ass. My mother thought so, too, I could tell; but I guess she was willing to put up with almost anything on this, her wedding day.

There were some fifty guests in all, including "a giggle of little girls" (Mr. Stenner's expression) who had been invited especially for me, friends of mine from the neighborhood where Dad still lived. There were four of them, including Julia D'Amiano. It felt strange seeing the D'Amianos at the wedding; they'd been friends of Mom's and Dad's before the split. Funny thing—I kept expecting to see *Dad* there. Expected him to walk through the door, shake hands with Mr. Stenner, kiss Mom on the cheek, do just what all the other guests were doing. It was weird. I

mean, I knew Dad hadn't been invited, knew in fact
that it would've been positively ridiculous to have invited him. Yet I expected him to be there.

"Which one is Mr. Stenner?" Julia asked.

"The one with the eyeglasses. Standing near the
fireplace."

"With the brown hair?"

"Yeah, and the eyeglasses."

"He's nice-looking," Julia said.

"You think so?" I said, and shrugged.

"Yeah," she said. "Does he beat you?"

"Mr. Stenner?" I said, and burst out laughing. "Of
course not!"

"Then maybe it won't be so bad," Julia said, and
shrugged. "Getting married again, I mean."

"Yeah," I said.

"Are you going to keep on living in this house?"

"We don't live in this house," I said.

"I thought you lived here."

"No. Mr. Stenner's lawyer lives here."

"Which one is he?"

"The one over there in the gray suit."

"The fat one?"

"Yeah, the pudgy one."

"Yeah," Julia said. "Him?"

"Yeah. His name is Arthur Randolph Knowles."

"How come they're getting married here, instead of
in a church?" Julia asked.

"Well, there'll be a minister and all," I said.

"Which one is the minister?"

"The one over there. Near the window."

"Why is his nose red?"

"Mom says he's a drunk."

"Why'd they hire a drunken minister?"

"He's not drunk *now*," I said. "And you don't hire
ministers. He married Mr. Knowles's son here in this
same house, and Mr. Knowles thought it would be appropriate if he did the job for Mom and Mr. Stenner,
too. Since it was the same house and all."

"Oh," Julia said, and hesitated for a long time. Then she said, "What does 'appropriate' mean?"

"Suitable," I said.

"Yeah," Julia said.

"Do you see that redhead over there?" I said.

"Which one?"

"In the low-cut dress."

"Yeah."

"She almost bit Mr. Stenner's finger off."

"Why?"

"Because he was pointing."

"Oh," Julia said. "Well, you shouldn't point. Here come two more people. Do they get flowers?"

"Yeah," I said. "They're my stepbrothers."

I was Luke and Jeff. They were supposed to get *red* flowers. This is the way it worked. Mom and Mr. Stenner had asked the florist to make up little nosegays for all the women guests who were members of the family or close friends. For the menfolk, there were red carnations and pink carnations. The red carnations went to family and the pink carnations went to close friends. Not everybody had a carnation or a nosegay. But nobody felt bad if they didn't get one, because they understood about family and close friends and all that. In fact, the only close friends who got carnations were Mr. Knowles, whose house the wedding was taking place in, and Mr. Flanders, who was Mr. Stenner's best man. Mom's maid of honor— or matron of honor, I guess—was Mrs. Alice Jackson, who'd gone to college with Mom, and who'd been her good friend ever since.

Luke and Jeff came in looking sort of stunned.

Jeff, the oldest son, the one who looked like Mrs. Stenner and had a beard, was wearing a rumpled corduroy suit and a shirt open at the throat. I remember thinking he shouldn't have looked so sloppy for his own father's wedding. Luke was wearing a plaid jacket, and gray flannel slacks, and a shirt and tie.

I said, "Hi," and they said, "Hi," and I handed

them both red carnations, and Jeff said, "What's this for?" and I said, 'You're supposed to put it in your lapel," and Luke said, "Here, let me help you, Jeff," and as they pinned on the flowers, they looked around the room. There were people there they knew, friends of their father from the old marriage, and people they'd met in the house we were renting, and of course Mr. Stenner's agent who they knew from when they were just this high.

I watched them as they walked deeper into the room. Mr. Knowles had put on some classical music, I heard it only as something in the background. They were shaking hands with people, these **tw**o boys who within the next half hour would become my legitimate stepbrothers. I could say to people, "These are my stepbrothers." I had always wanted a brother. When I was looking up all those names in the baby-name book, it was mostly boys' names I had looked up. I didn't know how I felt about having a pair of *step*brothers, though. They looked embarrassed. I suddenly understood what they were feeling. They were feeling, even though they were much older than I, even though they were almost grown up, they were feeling just what I was feeling. That the wrong two people were getting married today. It shouldn't have been Mom and Mr. Stenner. It should have been either Mom and Dad, or else Mr. Stenner and Joan Stenner, but it should not have been these two, it should not have been *my* mother and *their* father who were about to get married here today.

"Come on, Julia," I said. "Let's go outside."

We went outside to where Mr. Knowles had a swing hanging from a branch of an old oak tree, not a worn-out tire, but a real wooden swing that seemed to fit exactly the mood of the house. From the outside, the house itself looked like pictures I'd seen of houses in England. It didn't have a thatched roof or anything like that, but there were gables and leaded windows and huge chimneys. A rolling lawn ran from the back of the house to a stream below, and as Julia pushed me on the swing and I soared up into the sky, I could see a lonely horseman riding past far down on the other side of the stream. I thought back to that day when Mr. Stenner and I were walking around the hill, and he'd commented about the horse and rider, and then the swing came down again, and Julia pushed me up into the air, and I heard laughter, and then I heard Mr. Knowles's voice saying, "Of *course* I hired the horseman, got him from Central Casting," and there was more laughter, though I didn't get the joke.

I heard piano music coming from somewhere in the house, so I got off the swing, and Julia and I went to see if we could find out who was playing. In the music room we found the redheaded model who had almost bitten off Mr. Stenner's finger, and she was playing the bass hand to something while a man sitting alongside her on the bench was playing the melody. It was nice music, though not as good as rock. The wedding invitation had specified three P.M., and all of the guests were assembled by a quarter past—with the exception of one fashion editor who Mr. Stenner said was always late for everything. *She* arrived at three-thirty, and by three thirty-five the minister was ready to begin the ceremony. Mom came into the music room to tell everyone they were about to begin, and then she came to me and said, "Abby darling?" and I said, "Just a second, Mom," and she said, "Everybody? Please come," and smiled, and gestured toward the living room, and went out.

You've got to visualize this next scene.

Standing under the old oaken beams in the living room, the bay window streaming bright afternoon sunlight, Mom and Mr. Stenner heard the words and responded to them for the second time in each of their lives.

"Peter Stenner, will thou have this woman to be thy wedded wife, to live together in the holy estate of matrimony? Will thou love her, comfort her, honor and cherish her, in sickness and in health, prosperity and adversity, and forsaking all others, keep thee only unto her, so long as ye both shall live?"

"I will," he said.

"Lillith O'Neill, will thou have this man to be thy wedded husband, to live together in the holy estate of matrimony? Will thou love him, comfort him, honor and cherish him, in sickness and in health, prosperity and adversity, and forsaking all others, keep thee only unto him, so long as ye both shall live?"

"I will," she said.

"The wedding ring is the outward and visible sign of an inward bond," the minister said, "which unites two loyal hearts in endless love."

"In token of the vow made between us," Mr. Stenner said, "with this ring I thee wed."

"In token of the vow made between us," Mom said, "with this ring I thee wed."

"Forasmuch as Peter Stenner and Lillith O'Neill have consented together in holy wedlock, and have witnessed the same before God and this company, I pronounce that they are husband and wife together." The minister looked at them, and smiled, and said, "May God bless your union and grant to you the wisdom, strength, and love to nurture and sustain it forever. Amen."

Behind her, my mother heard Grandmother Lu's voice repeating the word "Amen," and then Mr. Stenner kissed Mom, and the minister leaned toward her and said in his gentle voice, "May I have the honor, Mrs. Stenner?" and kissed her on the cheek. Mom later told me she was thinking only *Mrs. Stenner, I am now Mrs. Stenner*, when suddenly she heard a shriek, and thought I'd hurt myself somehow, fallen from a chair, perhaps—had I been standing on a chair while watching the ceremony? And then it occurred to Mom that she hadn't seen me since several minutes *before* the ceremony, when she'd gone into the music room to tell me they were ready to start. She saw me pushing my way through the crowd now, clutching the nosegay Mr. Stenner had ordered specially for me, tiny pink roses and baby's breath. My face was contorted in agony, and tears were streaming down my cheeks.

"I *missed* it!" I said.

"What?" Mom said.

"What?" Mr. Stenner said.

"I missed the wedding!" I said, sobbing. "You didn't tell me the wedding was happening!"

"But I did tell you, darling. I came into the music room . . ."

"You didn't!" I said. "I missed the divorce, and now I missed the wedding, too!"

"Well," Mr. Stenner said, "if you missed it, you missed it." He took a fresh handkerchief from his pocket, dried my tears, and then said, "Now stop crying, or you'll miss the reception, too."

Mom watched him as he took my hand and walked to where his sons were standing. Both of them embraced him as he approached, and then Luke awkwardly patted me on the head.

9

Mr. Stenner began growing a beard shortly after the wedding, at about the same time Chiquita Banana came into my life. I was the one who nicknamed her Chiquita Banana. Her real name was Maria Victoria Valdez. Mr. Stenner had taught me the Chiquita Banana song, and I used to sing it around the house all the time. But I never thought I'd meet someone who was actually from South America, and who was my father's girlfriend besides. Well, not actually his girlfriend. I mean, they weren't too serious. I guess. But they were going out together. And maybe sleeping together, I'm not sure. Anyway, by the time I met her, they'd been seeing each other for quite some time. Maybe ever since Christmas. Or at least since Mom got the divorce in January. Come to think of it, that probably *was* when Dad started dating Chiquita Banana. Because in January he probably realized the marriage was really and truly over, red blob of wax on two red ribbons.

So one Saturday morning in June, Dad drove up to the house, everything in bloom, the forsythia bursting with yellow, the magnolia dripping pink petals on the lawn, the crocuses and day lilies and, oh, just everything in bloom, it was absolutely magnificent—and there was Chiquita Banana.

How to describe her?

Black hair.

Very white skin.

Eyes so brown they looked black.

Very curvaceous.

Yoke neck on her dress, *rah*-ther protuberant boobs.

Simpering smile on her face.

(Or was it fear?)

"Abby, I want you to meet Maria Victoria Valdez. Maria, this is my daughter."

"How do you do?"

(Should I curtsy?)

"How do you do, Abby?"

(She says it so that it sounds like "Ah-bee.")

"Well, get in, get in," my father says.

"What about my bag?"

"Oh, your bag. Right, right, your bag."

"I'll get it, Frank," Mr. Stenner says.

"That's okay, I've got it, Peter."

I hated her on sight.

I couldn't tell which I hated most—Mr. Stenner's beard or Chiquita Banana. To begin with, the beard wasn't a beard. Not like Jeff's beard. Not a real beard, not hair, not a full bushy *beard* on a person's face. It was just a scraggly collection of bristles that felt as if you'd walked into a porcupine whenever he gave you a hug.

"Please, Mr. Stenner," I begged him day and night, "*please* shave off the beard."

"I like the beard," he'd say, rubbing his hand over it. "Don't you like the beard, Lillith?"

"No," Mom would say.

"Gee, I like it," he'd say. "Give it a chance. It's only a few weeks old."

I guess he intended going through with it because when he went down to renew his passport, he didn't shave the beard, even though he knew they'd be taking a new picture of him. I went with him that day. The reason I went with him was because school had already ended at Hadley-Co, and I had nothing to do before we left for Europe.

We went for his passport on a Friday. Dad was

supposed to pick me up at five-thirty, after work, and it was about eleven in the morning when Mr. Stenner asked if I'd like to join him for lunch and for getting his new passport. I said I guessed it would be better than sitting around the house. The place we went to for his passport was the courthouse in White Plains. He filled out the application for renewal there, and then we went around the corner to have his picture taken. The photographer told us to come back for it in an hour, and that's when we went to lunch.

We had an interesting conversation during lunch.

I told him all about the time I'd been to Paris.

He said Mommy had told him a lot about that, too, about me going down the Champs Élysées doing a little dance with an umbrella. He told me that when Luke had been my age, he'd taken him and Jeff to London and the only thing Luke had wanted to buy was a bowler hat. He'd worn it all through England. He told me that every time he thought of me dancing down the Champs Élysées with my umbrella, he automatically thought of Luke wearing his bowler hat all through England. I didn't know what a bowler hat was. Mr. Stenner said it was a derby. Then he asked me how I liked my new stepbrothers.

"Well," I said, "no offense, Mr. Stenner, but I don't think they're *really* my stepbrothers yet."

"What do you mean?" he said.

"Well, I guess what it is . . . well, I don't think they like me very much."

"They're not used to having a sister," Mr. Stenner said.

"That may be part of it," I said, "but the other part is they just don't like me." I paused, and looked him straight in the eye, and then I said, "They don't like Mommy either."

He thought about this for what seemed like a long time. Then he nodded and said, "I guess you're right, Abby," and sighed.

"But I guess they'll begin to like us after a while," I said.

"I hope so," he said.

When we went back for the photograph, it was the laugh riot of the century. Even the photographer laughed. I begged Mr. Stenner to have another picture taken, but he thought this one was priceless and insisted that he would use it in his passport. The picture made him look like a punch-drunk fighter. He had this scraggly beard on his face, and the photographer snapped the picture just as he was blinking his eyes, so that he looked as if he was coming out of his corner for the tenth round. On the way back to the courthouse, I asked him why he hadn't taken his *own* picture for the passport, and Mr. Stenner said, "Bad subject."

"What do you mean?"

"I blink a lot."

Then he did something that embarrassed me to death.

"Bong!" he said, and immediately put up his fists like a fighter and came out of his corner bobbing and weaving and ducking his head and jabbing at an imaginary opponent, except that he wasn't in a prize-fight ring—he was on the main street of White Plains with people walking everywhere around us and thinking he had gone totally bananas. When he gave the picture to the clerk in the passport office, she looked up at him and said, "That's a winner, all right."

Driving back home from White Plains, I asked him something that had been bothering me for a while. "Mr. Stenner," I said, "what's the difference between a *step*brother and a *half*brother?"

"Well, if Mommy and I were to have a baby, a little boy, he'd be your half brother. Because you'd both have had the same mother but different fathers."

"*Are* you going to have a baby?" I asked immediately.

"We haven't really discussed it," Mr. Stenner said.

"But when you discuss it. *Then* will you have a baby?"

"I don't know."

"I don't want you to have a baby," I said.

"It's not something we vote on," Mr. Stenner said.

It was a good joke. I laughed at it.

If you encouraged him, he did outrageous things. In a restaurant, for example, he would order wine, and when the wine steward came and pulled the cork and poured a little of the wine into his glass to taste, Mr. Stenner would lift the glass to his lips, and take a sip of the wine, and roll it around on his tongue, and then pretend he'd been poisoned, clutching his throat and gasping for breath. Then he'd suddenly look up at the startled waiter, and smile, and say, "That's very nice, thank you."

Maria Victoria Valdez, on the other hand, had no sense of humor whatever. I told her a riddle I'd made up. The riddle was this: What did one fish say to the other fish after there'd been a long drought?

Maria looked at me and said, "What?"

"Long time no sea," I said.

Maria kept looking at me.

"Long time no *sea*," I said again.

She was still looking at me.

"Sea," I said. "S-E-A."

"Oh, it's a play on words, eh?" Maria said.

"Yeah," I said.

"That's very funny, Ah-bee," she said, but she didn't crack a smile.

"I guess it loses something in the translation," I said. That was one of Mr. Stenner's favorite lines. He'd say something he thought was hilariously funny, and if I didn't laugh he'd say, "I guess it loses something in the translation." Sometimes, just to tease him, I tried not to laugh at something that was really funny. Once, I almost wet my pants holding back the laughter. But Maria Victoria Valdez wasn't wetting her pants holding back any laughter. She just didn't find anything funny about "Long time no sea."

"Where will you be going on your trip, Ah-bee?" she asked.

She was making conversation. She didn't really care where I was going on my trip. All she cared about was the fact that I was going. Four weeks in Europe. Four weeks alone with Frank O'Neill. No bratty little daughter around telling incomprehensible riddles.

"We're going to Italy," I said.

"For four weeks?"

"Yes."

"All four weeks in Italy?"

"Yes. Mr. Stenner says there's lots to see in Italy. He says four weeks isn't enough time to see it all."

"This is a honeymoon?" Maria asked.

"Yes," I said.

"They are taking you on their honeymoon?"

"Well, they were living together for a long time before they got married, you know, it isn't as if this is such a big deal," I said.

My father looked up from where he was mixing Maria a drink. Maria tried a weak smile.

"Well, it's the truth," I said. "And anyway, they're married now. So what difference does it make?"

"Abby," my father said, "let's talk about something else, okay?"

"It was Maria who asked me about the trip."

"Yes, but not about the living arrangements of the past God knows how many months," my father said.

"What's wrong with the living arrangements?" I said. "The living arrangements are fine. I've got two rooms. I'll only have one room in the new house."

"When will you be moving into the new house?" Maria asked.

"When we get back from the honeymoon."

"In the fall?"

"Yeah, in September."

"What's the new house like?" my father asked.

"It's nice," I said. He was always doing that. First he would tell me *not* to talk about things, and then he would ask me questions about the very thing he had asked me not to talk about. Like our living arrangements.

"How many rooms are there?" he asked.

"Well, what difference does it make?" I said.

"Well, I'm an architect, I'm interested in houses," he said, and smiled at Maria. I was sure the smile meant something, but I didn't know what. I felt suddenly left out of things. Why was my father smiling at this strange person, this Chiquita Banana from Brazil, as if he was sharing the secrets of the world with *her*, when *I* was his daughter? Me! Abigail O'Neill! I was the one he should have been sharing the secrets with, whatever those secrets were.

"Are you going to sell this house or something?" I asked suddenly.

"No, no," my father said. "Whatever gave you that idea?"

"Well, why'd you just smile at Maria?"

"That had nothing to do with houses."

"What did it have to do with?"

"A private joke," my father said.

"What's the joke?" I said.

"You wouldn't understand it," my father said.

"Try me," I said, quoting Mr. Stenner.

"I'd rather not," my father said.

"Where in Italy will you be going?" Maria asked.

"I don't know where. Venice, I know, but the other cities . . . Rome, I think, is one of them."

"Venice is beautiful," Maria said. "Have you been to Venice, Frank?"

"Never," my father said.

"Perhaps we will go one day," Maria said.

"Will you take me?" I said.

"Ah, but you are going now," Maria said. "No?"

I hated her.

* * *

I have to admit there were a lot of changes after the wedding. I mean, in addition to Mr. Stenner's dumb beard.

"Hey, look at this, will you?" he'd say. "It's got red hairs in it, will you look at it?"

"Those are blond."

"Red! Look at them, Abby!"

"Mr. Stenner . . . shave it off, okay?"

The changes took place in all of us. They were subtle changes, maybe, but they were also very important ones. For example, Mom seeing her name on her own stationery made a difference: *Lillith Stenner*, and under it, the address of the new house we'd bought. It wasn't just that the house we were moving into had been *bought* rather than rented, it was that *we* had bought it. Not just Mr. Stenner. Us. *All* of us. We all had a stake in it. In the same way that we all knew the house we'd been living in was *not* ours—the cavalry officer on the wall never allowed us to forget that simple fact—we also knew that the house we'd be moving to in the fall *was* ours. Mom and Mr. Stenner had shown me the deed, it had both their names on it: "Peter and Lillith Stenner, husband and wife." Seeing the deed made me sort of wish *my* name was Abigail Stenner instead of Abigail O'Neill.

I know that sounds like I was being a traitor to my real father, and actually, whenever I had a thought like that, I did feel as if I were betraying him. But at the same time, I felt that now that Mom and Mr. Stenner were married, and we were sort of a family, with Mom being Lillith Stenner and all—well, it just sometimes seemed to me that it would be more natural if I were Abigail Stenner. If only for the sake of avoiding confusion.

Father's Day was a real hassle.

Father's Day came in June, and this particular Father's Day fell on a Sunday two weeks before we were supposed to leave for Europe. This was the first time I'd ever had two fathers to worry about, a real father and a stepfather. The main problem was where to spend Father's Day. Should I spend it at home (Mr. Mauley's house), or should I spend it away from home (Dad's house)? The choice seemed obvious to me. Of course I would spend Father's Day at Dad's house. He was my father, right? My real father. My natural father. But at the same time, I didn't want to hurt Mr. Stenner's feelings. Because I was beginning to think of him as a good man. Which is what Mom had told me he was.

So here was Father's Day, and Mom had taken me out on the Tuesday before, mainly to shop for clothes I would need in Italy because I seemed to be suddenly outgrowing things in leaps and bounds, but also to buy presents for the real father over there and the fake father over here. For the real one—Frank O'Neill himself, world's greatest architect—I bought a striped silk tie that cost four dollars and thirty-six cents with the tax, and I made up a poem that I typed on Mom's typewriter. This is what the poem looked like:

> To My Father
> I love you, Dad, in every way,
> I love you more than I can say.
> I want to wish you, if I may,
> A peaceful, happy Father's Day.
>
> > Love,
> > Abby

For the fake one—Peter Stenner, world's greatest fashion photographer, punch-drunk fighter, and punster—I bought a metal statue of the Empire State Building, and I cut out a picture of a gorilla from a magazine, and I Scotch-taped it to the top of the Empire State Building, and on a little piece of white paper I hand-lettered:

YOU'RE THE KING, KONG!
HAPPY FATHER'S DAY.

ABBY

I knew he'd get the joke because we'd watched *King Kong* on television together only a few weeks before. Mom told me it was appropriate for me to visit my father on Father's Day, even though it wasn't one of the weekends I was supposed to be visiting him. The calendar in our house was marked with Abigail here" or "Abigail Frank's" on alternating weekends. It got confusing around holiday time, when all the rules were canceled. Speaking of rules, Mr. Stenner had taken down the Rules List the day after the wedding. When I asked him how come, he just shrugged and said, "We don't need them anymore, do we?" Anyway, on Father's Day, at about twelve noon, my father's car came driving up to the front of the house, but my father wasn't driving it. Instead, Chiquita Banana was behind the wheel.

"Where's Dad?" I said.

"He's sick," she said.

"Sick?" Mom said. I could see the look of alarm in her eyes. What did the poor man have? Something communicable? Would Abigail O'Neill come back from a visit to her father with some incurable Asian disease?

"Just a head cold," Chiquita Banana said. "But he didn't think he should leave the house."

"I don't want Abby catching a cold," Mom said. "We're leaving for Europe in two weeks . . ."

"It makes no difference to me," Chiquita said flatly, "whether she visits her father or not. He asked me to come for her."

"I see," Mom said.

"Well," Mr. Stenner said, "if it makes no difference to you, it makes a lot of difference to us. We can't afford to have Abby catch whatever it is Frank has."

"Gee," I said, "I won't catch it."

"I'd better call your father," Mom said.

This was another subtle difference, by the way. After the wedding, Mom never referred to my father as "Dad" anymore. In the old days, she would have said, "I'd better call Dad." Now she said, "I'd better call your father."

Which she went to do while we all waited in the driveway.

"What part of Brazil are you from?" Mr. Stenner asked our Latin American neighbor.

"Rio," she said.

"I shot some stuff for *Vogue* down there once," Mr. Stenner said.

"Vogue?" she said.

"The magazine," he said.

"Ah, *Vogue*," she said. "The magazine."

Mom came out of the house.

"Well?" I said.

"Your father and I think it might be best for you to stay home today," she said.

"But it's Father's Day!" I said.

"You can see him next week, Abby," Mom said.

"Next week isn't Father's Day!" I said.

"Abby, we don't want you catching cold," Mom said.

"You just don't want me to spent Father's Day with Dad!" I said.

"Abby, that isn't . . ."

"For*get* it!" I said, and stormed into the house.

It wasn't the same spending Father's Day with him a week after Father's Day. His cold was gone by then, but so was the holiday. I gave him the tie, and he said he liked it very much. Before I left him, he made me promise to write him every day from Italy, if only a postcard.

Two days before we left, Mr. Stenner shaved off the beard.

10

The thing Mom forgot to do was get her name changed in her passport.

At the last minute, she remembered that in her passport she was still Lillith O'Neill. So Mr. Stenner had a photocopy made of their marriage certificate, and he stapled *that* into the back of her passport—"Not that it'll make any difference," he said.

The way he explained it, in Italy there were so many complications with forms and papers that the average Italian always figured there'd been some error and simply shrugged it off. My passport read *Abigail O'Neill*. Mom's passport read *Lillith O'Neill*. When Mr. Stenner registered us in the Milan hotel as Mr. and Mrs. Peter Stenner, and daughter," the clerk didn't look at all surprised. The different names on the passports didn't necessarily mean the Stenners, or the O'Neills, or *whoever*, were not a family. An error in the papers, no doubt. They looked like a family, they'd registered as a family, so perhaps that made them a family. Or at least, that's the way Mr. Stenner explained the Italian attitude, and I think he was right.

The first thing I did in the lobby was go over to where they had a rack of postcards. I bought four postcards from my Italian allowance. In Italy, I was supposed to get the equivalent in Italian money of five dollars a week to spend on myself and on souvenirs.

I bought the postcards for Dad, of course.

To send to Dad.

Mr. Stenner was still at the desk, signing in, and asking the clerk whether it was necessary to leave his camera in the hotel vault. The clerk, in perfect English, said that it might be a good idea, if it would not inconvenience the *signore*. The *signore* was Mr. Stenner. In Italy, the word for "mister" or "sir" was *signore* and the word for "Mrs." or "madam" was *signora*. But the plural of *signore* was *signori*, and the plural of *signora* was *signore*. So you had to be careful when you went to the toilet, otherwise you could walk into the wrong place. In France, when I was there with my mother and my father, we went to some towns where the men and women used the *same* bathroom, would you believe it? I was washing my hands at the sink in one of those bathrooms—this was in the Loire Valley, when we were looking at all the castles— and a *man* came out of one of the stalls! I almost dropped dead right on thes pot. "*Bonjour, mademoiselle,*" he said to me, and smiled, and proceeded to wash his hands at the sink next to mine.

In France, when I took the trip with Mom and Dad, I slept in the same room with them wherever we stayed. I wanted to do that in Italy, too, with Mom and Mr. Stenner, but he said absolutely not.

"Why not?" I said.

"Because we all need privacy," he said.

"It's cheaper with just one room."

"We can afford two rooms," he said.

"Then they have to be right alongside each other, and there has to be a door between them, okay?" I said.

"We'll ask for connecting rooms. If we can get them, fine. If not, we'll have to take what we can get."

"Well, I don't want to be on a different floor."

"Why not?"

"Because I'd be afraid."

"Of what?"

"That somebody would kidnap me."

"If somebody kidnaps you, just yell and I'll come rescue you," he said, and smiled.

That's what I was really worried about, you see. That he wouldn't come rescue me. Because he wasn't my real father. I knew my real father would throw himself in front of a bus for me, but Mr. Stenner was only my stepfather. With your natural father you could assume that he and your mother wanted to have a baby, and got together, you know, and had one nine months later. But with your stepfather, you had to assume that what he wanted was to marry your mother. Period. The rest came along with the deal. If he wanted to marry Mom, well—you see, there was this gorgeous little eleven-year-old brat who was part of the bargain. You took one, you automatically got the other.

So why should he worry if anybody kidnapped me?

Why should he come to the rescue?

He was still at the desk when I walked over from the postcard rack. In the middle of what he was saying, I asked, "Are they connecting?"

"Just a minute, Abby," he said. To the clerk, he said, "Is someone always here at the desk?"

"Oh, *yes*, sir," the clerk said.

"Mr. Stenner? Are they . . ."

"Then perhaps I could just leave the camera in my box," he said. "Instead of going through the business of opening the vault each time."

"As you wish, *signore*," the clerk said.

"Mr. Stenner, are they connecting?"

"Yes," he said. "They're connecting, Abby."

He was silent all the way up in the elevator. The rooms were really terrific. I wanted the biggest one, which had a little balcony outside the window, but Mom said the other one was mine.

"How come you get the best one?" I said.

"In this case, second best is only magnificent," Mom said.

"Yeah, but . . ."

"When *you* take *your* daughter to Italy," Mr. Stenner said, "you and your husband can have the biggest room for yourselves, okay? Meanwhile, Abby, let me tell you something about *this* trip, okay?"

"Sure," I said. "What?"

I didn't know he was about to yell at me. In fact, he didn't yell at me. That is, he didn't raise his voice. But there was no question about the fact that I was being bawled out for something I didn't even know I'd done. Flabbergasted, I listened to him.

"I told you before we left home," he said, "that we'd requested connecting rooms in all the hotels. I also told you we'd take whatever was available because we'd made our plans late, and this was the height of the tourist season. Now, Abby, when I'm talking to a desk clerk, I want you to keep out of it. I don't want you hanging around the registration desk while I'm giving the man our passports, and filling out cards, and what-have-you. And I especially don't want you interrupting with stupid questions about whether or not the rooms are connecting."

"I don't think that's a stupid question," I said. "It happens to be very important to me. Whether or not the rooms are connecting."

"I understand that. It's important to us, too. I can only tell you that the first question I asked the clerk was whether or not the rooms were connecting, and he assured me they were. If he'd told me they weren't, I would have asked whether or not it was possible to get connecting rooms, and if not, I would have asked for at least adjoining rooms. And if I couldn't have got any of those, only *then* would I have settled for a room down the hall or, as a last resort, on another floor of the hotel. The point is I can handle it myself, Abby, I don't need any assistance from an eleven-year-old girl. From now on, keep out of it. I am perfectly capable of registering my own family."

"Nobody was trying to help you register," I said.

"And I didn't know you'd asked the clerk about connecting rooms because, if you didn't notice, I was buying some postcards."

"I did notice," Mr. Stenner said. "And I'm also noticing the look on your face right this minute, and I'm hearing the tone of your voice, and I can't say I appreciate either. Mom and I told you this vacation was important to us. We've been through a lot in the past several months, and now we want to relax. Italy is a beautiful country, the people here are marvelous, the food is delicious. All I want is for us to enjoy ourselves. We're not going to enjoy ourselves if you try to run the show."

"I wasn't trying to run the show."

"You didn't trust me," he said.

"I trusted you," I said.

That was a lie, of course. I hadn't trusted him. I just didn't think he cared whether the rooms were connecting, or adjoining, or across the hall from each other, or down the hall, or three floors apart, or separated by the Atlantic Ocean or the continent of Africa. I just didn't think he gave a damn.

"You can trust me," he said.

"I can trust you to yell at me for nothing," I said.

"Let's all take a nap now," he said. "We're exhausted, we're . . ."

"I'm not exhausted," I said. "I want to write some cards to Dad."

"Fine," he said, and went into his own room, and closed and locked the door behind him. Through the closed door, I could hear him and Mom talking.

"Was I too rough on her?" he asked.

"No," Mom said.

"I just wanted to get it straight from the beginning, Lil."

"You did the right thing."

"It *is* a hassle coming into a hotel, and when she stands around sniping . . ."

"I know, darling."

"I'm tired," he said. "Let's get some sleep."

On the card to my father, I wrote:

> Dear Dad,
> I miss you. I wish I were home
> with you.
> Love and kisses.
>
> > Your   daughter,
> > Abby
>
> P.S. A hundred million hugs and kisses.
> > I love you.

At about five o'clock that afternoon, Mr. Stenner popped into the room and cheerfully said, "Everybody *up*, time to get *up!*"

I opened my eyes and blinked at him.

"Let's go, Abby, time to see Milan!"

"I don't want to see Milan," I said.

"You don't? You came all the way to Italy, and you don't want to see Milan?"

"That's right," I said.

"Well, Milan wants to see you," he said, and grinned, and looked at his watch, and said, "It's almost five past five. I'll give you ten minutes to get up, and wash your face, and put on a pretty dress, and then off we go to the Galleria for an early evening drink and a stroll."

"What's the Galleria?" I asked.

"It's an arcade enclosed entirely in glass, it's like nothing you've ever seen in your life, you cutie pie! So pop out of bed and let's get going!"

"Is Mom out of bed yet?"

"Mom is out of bed and at this very moment soaking in the bathtub. Mom *has* in fact been in the bathtub for the past ten minutes, and I'm about to hustle her out." He looked at his watch again. "You have exactly nine minutes and ten seconds."

"Mr. Stenner?" I said.

"Yes?"

"I'm sorry about what happened in the lobby."

"That's ancient history," he said. "But do you understand why I yelled at you, Abby?"

"I guess," I said.

"Okay, let's move it!" he said, and grinned again, and went out of the room.

The Galleria was absolutely fantastic.

He was right.

I'd never seen anything like it in my life. What it was, they had built this structure in the shape of a cross and then covered it over with glass so that the sun shone down onto the tiled floors. A lot of things in Italy are tiled, but I didn't know that when we first got to Milan. All I knew was that I was inside this marvelous arcade lined with restaurants and shops, and the sun was shining down on us from above, and breezes were blowing through from the various entrances at the four ends of the cross.

We sat at a table and watched the people go by. The trouble hadn't started yet, we were so far having a pretty good time, despite what had happened in the lobby and the little bawling-out I'd got afterward. Mr. Stenner was staring at my wrist. Or, to be more exact, he was staring at the ragged piece of yarn I'd knotted around it.

"What's that?" he said.

"It's a forever."

"What's a forever?"

"It's a thing you tie around your wrist and you keep wearing it forever."

"For*ever*?"

"Well, until it falls off. It's supposed to bring good luck."

"Mm," he said, and kept staring at it very thoughtfully.

"What's the matter?" I said.

"Nothing," he said, "nothing," and shrugged and

smiled, and asked if I felt like trying a little game he and the boys used to play when they were small and he'd taken them to Europe. I said, "Sure, what's the game?" and he explained that all we had to do was look at the people passing by and—*before* we heard them talking—try to guess what nationality they were. He said it wasn't as easy as I thought it might be because people from foreign countries often bought clothes in the country they were visiting, and looked exactly like the citizens of that country.

We started playing the game.

I said, "Here come two Americans," but when they got closer, the man and the woman were speaking a language even *I* knew was German. Mom guessed that the next people coming toward us were French— a man, his wife, and their son and daughter. As it turned out, she was right. I recognized the language as soon as they came close. When Mr. Stenner asked her how she'd known, she said it was because Frenchmen always knotted the sleeves of their sweaters around their waists or their necks. He said he hadn't noticed that before, and then he spotted a man coming along with his sweater sleeves knotted around his waist, and he guessed the man was French, but the man greeted another man in fluent Italian, so that was that. I saw an Oriental man and woman coming along, and I whispered, "They're Japanese. Or Chinese." But as they passed the table, we heard them talking in English about San Francisco.

It really was a difficult game.

Mr. Stenner had ordered for me what he called "an Italian Shirley Temple," a drink that was tall and green and frothy and floating with lemon slices. He got up from the table now, and began taking pictures of me as I nibbled at the lemon slices, my mouth puckered, clearing out the pulp until I was holding only a pair of miniature rind wheels, which I held up alongside my face.

Click, the camera shutter went.

"Can we send copies of these to Daddy?" I asked, and I saw Mr. Stenner's face fall. He sat down quickly, closed the cover on his camera case, and ordered a double Scotch on the rocks.

"What's the matter?" I asked.

"Nothing," he said.

"All I said . . ."

"I heard what you said."

"Well, what's so wrong about that? All I want is some copies for Daddy. If you're worried about how much they'll cost, I'll pay for them from my allowance."

Mr. Stenner said nothing. Mom watched him.

"Well?" I said.

"No," he said.

"Why not?"

"These are *our* pictures," he said.

"Nobody said they weren't."

"Exclusively ours," he said.

"What's exclusively?"

"For *our* album. *Our* family album. I don't want to send prints to your father, okay?"

"Then I don't want to *be* in the album, okay?" I said.

"Okay," he said.

"And don't take any more pictures of me, okay?"

"Okay."

"Okay," I said.

On the roof of Il Duomo, he took pictures of Mom coming through a stone archway, a blue-hooded telescope in the foreground. He took a picture of her standing alongside a column with winged angels on it, and another of her against a background of scaffolding that seemed starkly modern in contrast to the gingerbread statuary. He took pictures of the black-and-white-tiled square below. He even took pictures of the parking lot across the street from the cathedral, shooting down at the red, and blue, and white cars that from above looked like miniature toys.

At the Cenacolo Vinciano, where we went to see Leonardo's fresco, he took a picture of Mom sitting on one of the high wooden benches, the rubbed walnut glowing behind her. And in the park later, he took pictures of some kids watching an outdoor Punch-and-Judy show, and pictures of some men studying a gambler who was playing a shell game, and even pictures of goldfish in a pond. But he did not take any more pictures of me.

Lying awake in bed that night, I heard them whispering next door.

"I'm not trying to punish her, Lil," he said.

"I know that."

"It makes me angry, though . . ."

"The way she . . ."

"Her constant little reminders that I'm not her father. I know I'm not her father! All I'm trying to be is her *step*father!"

"You're very good with her, Peter. I couldn't have asked for . . ."

"Oh, the hell with that, Lillith. Who cares how good I am with her? She doesn't care, that's for sure."

"She does, Peter. It's just . . ."

"It's just she's afraid I'm going to steal her from her precious Daddy. She'd like to pretend the divorce never happened and the wedding never happened, and everything is just the same as . . . and what was *that* supposed to be, would you please tell me? How could she have missed the wedding? I saw you going in there to get her, she couldn't have missed the wedding unless she *wanted* to miss it."

"I suppose she did want to miss it," Mom said.

"And why did he have to call the house just as we were leaving for the airport?" Mr. Stenner asked. "He'd said good-bye to her the night before, hadn't he? So why'd he have to call again in the morning? We weren't taking her to a Siberian prison camp, we were taking her to Italy for a vacation! Did you hear her on the telephone? She sounded like Camille on her deathbed. I think half of it is phony, Lil. I think she puts on a big act for him and a bigger act for us."

"No, I think she's genuinely unhappy," Mom said.

"Why should she be? I've tried every damn . . ."

"Have you ever tried *loving* her?"

"I'm not sure I *do* love her."

"Sometimes, Peter, you sound as if you hate her," Mom said.

"Sometimes I do," he said.

11

On the train to Venice, he hardly said a word to me. He was sitting there reading his Italian grammars for half the trip, and then he put the books aside with a sigh, and stared out the window. In a little while, he got up from his seat and went down the aisle, to the toilet I supposed. I turned to Mom and said, "What's the matter with him this morning?" I knew what was the matter with him, of course; I'd overheard their conversation the night before. He hated me because I loved my father, that's what was the matter with him.

"Who," Mom said, spacing the words evenly, "is *him?*"

"Him," I said. "Mr. Stenner."

"Nothing is the matter with Mr. Stenner," Mom said. "Mr. Stenner is fine."

When he came back to his seat, I said, "Do you know what the concierge said to me this morning?"

"The hall porter," Mr. Stenner corrected. "In France, he's the concierge. In Italy, he's . . ."

"Daddy told me I should call him the concierge."

"Oh? When did he tell you that?"

"Before we left."

"Is that why he phoned the house that morning? To make sure you knew what to call the concierge?"

"No, he phoned to say good-bye. But before that . . ."

"Anyway, he's not called a concierge, he's called a hall porter."

"That's not what Daddy said."

"Has Daddy ever been to Italy?"

"No, but . . ."

"Then tell Daddy not to tell *me* what the hall porter is called in Italy, okay? As a matter of fact, tell Daddy to mind his own business, and we'll all get along much . . ."

"I am Daddy's business," I said.

"Fine," Mr. Stenner said.

"Anyway, would you like to hear what he said to me? The concierge or the hall porter or whatever you . . ."

"It's the hall porter."

"All *right*, it's the hall porter, all right? He asked me where my father was."

"Did you tell him your father was home in the United States, pining for his darling daughter?"

"He meant you," I said.

"I'm not your father," he said. "We all know that."

"But you *are* my stepfather. I felt sort of dumb. I didn't know what to say to him."

"What did you say to him?"

"I said you were upstairs in the room."

In Venice, he began taking pictures of me again.

There were pigeons strutting all over the square, flying in the sky overhead, lofting in the spires of the church and in the arched windows above the arcades. For a hundred lire, you could buy a rolled newspaper cone filled with feed, and I bought a coneful now with money Mr. Stenner had given me. He was wearing a leather cap he'd bought in Milan, which he said made him feel more Italian, and which was sort of tilted over one eye. I walked out into the middle of the square and tried to tempt some pigeons into accepting food from the palm of my hand.

Piazza San Marco means "St. Mark's Square" in Italian, and it's this huge square, I would guess about the size of a football field. Or if it isn't that big it cer-

tainly *feels* that big. And there are outdoor tables on
the two long sides of the square—it isn't really a
square, it's a rectangle—and there I was in the middle
of it trying to feed the pigeons, and none of them
would eat anything. So I went back to the table just
as the waiter was bringing the drinks Mr. Stenner had
ordered for all of us. I sipped a little of my Coke, and
said, "It's hot out there, Mr. Stenner. Do you think I
could borrow your hat? To keep the sun off?"

"Sure," he said, and took the cap from his head, and
handed it to me. The cap was made of the softest
glove leather, with a wide curving bill and a puffed
crown. It was maybe three sizes too large for me, but
I pulled it over my hair anyway, and went out to try
with the pigeons again. Mr. Stenner was sipping at his
drink and watching me as I stalked a bird across the
square. Then I dropped to one knee, and shook some
feed into the palm of my right hand, and held the feed
out to the bird. The bird watched me, but didn't come
anywhere near. Patiently, I crouched and waited for
him to come to my outstretched hand.

Mr. Stenner later told me it was only his own sense
of professionalism that caused him to rise so suddenly;
the combination of blond little me with the beige cap
pulled down over my long, straight hair, and the gray
pigeon waddling toward the feed on my open palm—
these were irresistible to his photographer's eye. I
didn't even see him approaching. I was still crouched,
one knee on the ground, the other knee supporting
my extended arm. A little Italian girl with close-
cropped black hair, wearing a blouse embroidered
with a flower design, and a red-and-white-check skirt,
and white knee socks, and black high-topped shoes,
stopped beside me and watched me and the bird.

The pigeon took two small steps toward my hand,
examined the dried green peas and yellow triangles of
corn on my palm, and took a timid peck at the feed. I
was totally unaware of Mr. Stenner crouched not five
feet away from me, his shutter clicking frantically as

two, and then three pigeons waddled over to share in the loot. I got to my feet to pour more feed from the rolled newspaper into my hand, and the birds fluttered up toward the cone, one of them perching on its rim, another perching on my shoulder, a third perching on top of my head. I opened my eyes wide in astonishment, and then I began giggling.

The way Mom tells it, she was watching the whole episode from where she sat at the little round table across the square. She saw Mr. Stenner circling me, constantly cocking the shutter, pressing the shutter release, cocking it again, focusing, snapping. In those brief intervals when the camera momentarily left his eye, Mom saw that he was smiling. I was surrounded by a cloud of fluttering, flapping pigeons and grinning from ear to ear when I finally realized he was taking pictures of me. Mom says I turned away in embarrassment and started to say, "Oh, Da . . ." and cut myself short.

But my excited voice had carried clear across the square to where she was sitting.

I guess the reason he thought we were starting to be such good friends was his hat. I simply refused to take off his hat. He asked me if he might have it back, but I pleaded and begged and cajoled until he promised I could continue wearing it—but only till we got to Rome.

"Why only till Rome?" I asked.

"Because in Rome you'll have something else to . . . well, you'll just have something else."

"What do you mean? What does he mean, Mom?"

"I don't know," Mom said. "Ask *him*."

"What, Mr. Stenner?"

"Well, your birthday's coming," he said.

"Did you buy me a hat like yours for my birthday?"

"Nope."

"What *did* you buy me?"

"Nothing."

"Then what do you mean, I'll have something else in Rome?"

"I'm going to buy it when we get to Rome. If I can find it there."

"But it's not a hat?"

"Nope."

"What is it then?"

"A secret."

"What does it start with?"

"F," he said.

"F? Nothing starts with F," I said, and giggled. "Mommy, make him tell me what it is."

"Then it won't be a secret anymore," Mom said.

"If you tell me your secret, I'll tell you mine," I said.

"Nope," he said.

"Don't you want to know my secret?"

"Sure," he said.

"Then let's swap secrets."

"No, I don't want to spoil your birthday surprise."

"Tell me what it is, Mr. Stenner. Please?"

"Nope."

"Pretty please?"

"Nope."

"Does it start with F in Italian, or in English?"

"In English."

"Are you sure? Because if it's an Italian word, then that's cheating."

"It's an English word."

"Because I can't talk Italian very well. Are you sure it's English?"

"Yes, it's English."

"F," I said.

"F," he repeated.

"Is it a feather?"

"A feather? Why would I want to buy you a feather?"

"So I can tickle myself," I said, and giggled. "*Is* it a feather?"

"No," he said.

"Thank God!" I said. "Is it flowers? Are you going to get me a bouquet of flowers?"

"No."

"Then what is it? Is it a frying pan?"

"A frying pan!" he said, and we both burst out laughing.

"Come on, Mr. Stenner, please tell me."

"You'll have to wait till the sixteenth," he said.

"That's *forever*," I said.

"That's right," he said, and winked at Mom.

I would not let up. I think he was beginning to feel sorry he'd even mentioned the gift, while at the same time dreading the possibility that he might not be able to find it in Rome. Meanwhile, I would not part with the hat. I loved that hat! In the rented car on the way to Rimini, I wore the hat. And in the restaurant where we stopped for lunch, I wore the hat. And at the Rimini hotel, I was still wearing the hat as he and I sat together in the garden, waiting for Mom, who was upstairs dressing for dinner. I asked him to please order me an Italian Shirley Temple, and then we sat sipping our separate drinks in the gathering dusk. The floor of the terrace was paved with white tile, and there were royal blue tablecloths on the round metal tables. Mr. Stenner was never without one or another of his cameras hanging around his neck, and I said to him now, "This would make a good shot from upstairs. From one of our rooms. Looking down at all the blue circles against the white."

"Yes," he said, and nodded. "It would."

"Like the picture you took from the roof of the church in Milan," I said. "Of the automobiles down below. Do you remember?"

"Yes."

"That was the day you wouldn't take *my* picture," I said.

"Yes, I remember."

"Just because I asked you to have some copies made for Daddy."

"Mm," he said.

"You don't have to be so jealous all the time, you know."

"What?" he said.

"You," I said. "Of Daddy."

"What makes you think I'm jealous?"

"Because you are. But you don't have to be. I know you're my stepfather."

"I'm certainly happy to hear that," he said.

"Oh, sure," I said. "What do people call their stepfathers, anyway?"

"I don't know," he said.

"Because I feel sort of dumb calling you 'Mr. Stenner.' "

"Why's that?" he asked.

"I don't know," I said and shrugged. "In the lobby and all. And when we were in the restaurant. Do you remember when we stopped for lunch on the way here?"

'Yes?"

"Well, the waiter understood English, and he heard me calling you 'Mr. Stenner,' and I could tell he was puzzled. You see, he knew you and Mommy were married because he could see you were both wearing the same wedding bands, so if you were married and here's a girl traveling with you, then the girl ought to be your daughter, right? So why was I calling you 'Mr. Stenner'? That's what the waiter must've been wondering."

"Probably."

"What are you going to buy me in Rome?" I said. "A fencing thing?"

"What's a fencing thing?" he asked.

"What you fence with," I said. "What the kids on the fencing team at school fence with."

"A foil, do you mean?"

"Right! That begins with an F, doesn't it? Is it a foil?"

"Nope. And it's not a fedora, either."

"What's a fedora?"

"A hat."

"Well, you already *told* me you weren't going to buy a hat. What is it, I'm dying to know. Is it a fig?"

"You had a fig at lunch today."

"I know, but are you buying me another fig? As a joke?"

"Would I joke about your twelfth birthday?" he asked.

"I don't know," I said, and shrugged again. "I love the sound of the ocean, don't you?"

"Yes," he said.

"Let's have a drink every night, okay? While we're waiting for Mommy to get dressed."

"Only if we're ready before she is," he said.

"Yes, only if we're ready, okay?"

"Okay," he said.

"Is it a fiddle?" I asked. "Are you going to buy me a fiddle?"

"No," he said.

"Then what? A fire engine?"

It was nice there on the terrace.

12

The hotel in Florence was about five minutes outside the city itself, perched on the edge of the Arno River. It had windows overlooking gardens and a pool on one side, and on the other an awninged outdoor restaurant and the river below. In the lobby of the hotel, Mr. Stenner translated for me an Italian sign that indicated how high the water had risen during the flood several years back. I looked at the mark on the sign and said, "You mean right here in the lobby?"

"That's right," Mr. Stenner said.

"Wow!" I said. "Aren't you glad we weren't here *then?*"

"I was here just the year before that," he said.

"This same place?"

"Yes."

"With the boys?"

"Yes."

"And with Mrs. Stenner?"

"Right," he said.

"Wrong!" I said, and grinned. "Mommy's Mrs. Stenner. The other Mrs. Stenner isn't Mrs. Stenner anymore." I paused. "Is she?" I asked.

"No," he said.

"Good," I said.

I found it difficult to make friends.

I don't think it had anything to do with the divorce. I think I was just kind of shy. Not so much with grown-ups, but definitely with kids. We would come back from the city of Florence, and I'd mope around the pool, listening to the kids splashing at the other end of it, and wishing I could join them. The pool was about fifteen feet long—it was almost impossible to *avoid* making friends with any other kids who were in the pool, but I sure managed. Until Mr. Stenner popped into the water one day. Popped in? He *jumped* right into the middle of a game a girl and her brother were playing.

Here were these two kids splashing around and yelling at each other, the girl about seven and the boy about ten. And all of a sudden this big gangling oaf landed right in the middle of what they were doing, and disappeared under the surface of the water, and then came up an instant later squirting water out of his mouth like a fountain and looking stupid as could be.

"Hi, kids," he said. "I'm Peter Stenner."

"Hi," the girl said.

"Hi," the boy said.

They weren't used to grown-ups being so dumb, you could tell that. But they were smiling. They liked his trying to be friendly with them.

"What's your name?" he asked the girl.

"Marlene," she said.

"Yeah?" he said. "Hi, Marlene. And what's your name?" he asked the boy.

"Tommy," the boy said.

"You guys met Abby yet? Abby, come meet Tommy and Marlene."

"Hi," I mumbled.

"Hi," Marlene said.

"Hi," Tommy said.

"What's that game you're playing?" Mr. Stenner asked.

"It's a game we made up," Tommy said. "It's you have to swim to *that* side and touch it with both hands, and then you have to turn around, and kick off, and come back to *this* side and touch it with both hands, too."

"Who wins?" Mr. Stenner asked.

"Nobody wins," Tommy said. "It's just a game we made up."

"Mind if Abby and I play it with you?"

"Come on," Marlene said. "But you have to touch the sides with *both* hands."

"It's not as easy as it looks, you know," Tommy said gravely.

That's how I got to meet Tommy and Marlene.

At dinner that night, when I saw Mr. Stenner raise his glass, I knew he was about to propose a toast, and I lifted my glass too. In Italy, they allowed me to have a little wine with dinner, it's really a quite civilized country. I mean, not only did Mom and Mr. Stenner allow me to have wine, but the people running the restaurants never objected to it, in fact seemed to encourage it.

"Will *la ragazzina* have a little wine, too, *signore?*" the waiter always asked, and then set a sparkling wineglass on the table before me. In America, you just *try* to sneak a little glass of wine to your daughter without her showing an ID card and a birth certificate and a driver's license and a passport and a vaccination mark—wow! People pop out of the kitchen, the manager runs over to the table, the headwaiter takes a fit, the FBI comes through the door with drawn pistols and automatic machine guns . . . forget it.

"I'd like to say," Mr. Stenner said, "that I love being here in this time and in this place with these two people. Lil," he said, and clinked his glass against hers, and then said, "Abby," and clinked his glass against mine. "It's good," he said, and nodded, but he hadn't sipped the wine yet, and I knew he wasn't talking about that.

* * *

The Ponte Vecchio was packed with tourists, of course, and all of them had cameras. Whatever their nationality, they had cameras. Big cameras, little cameras, simple cameras, complicated cameras, cheap cameras, expensive cameras. They all had cameras, and they were all taking pictures. Pictures of wives, husbands, children, friends, aunts, uncles. Mr. Stenner was sure the family albums of the world were full of bad snapshots of people posing uncomfortably in front of statues of men whose names they couldn't pronounce, smiling stiffly and squinting into the sun. "You must always take a picture with the sun over your left shoulder," his uncle used to tell him when he was a boy. His uncle was an accountant, but no matter—"Always over the left shoulder, Peter."

In Florence, on the Ponte Vecchio, Mr. Stenner's idea was to take pictures of people taking pictures.

He took the first of these at the end of the street, where the barricades were set up. A fat woman in a flowered dress was kneeling, one knee on the sidewalk, taking a picture of her small son or grandson who was eating a chocolate ice-cream cone and spilling half of it down his shirt front. As Mr. Stenner took the picture, I said, "What are you doing?" and he whispered, "Shhh," and I immediately got the idea. He was taking a picture of a person taking a picture. In that minute, I became a scout for him.

By the end of the day, he'd shot a full roll—thirty-six exposures—of people taking pictures. Of those thirty-six, I scouted at least twenty for him, tugging at his sleeve, glancing to where somebody was about to click a shutter—a man taking a picture of his wife holding their baby up against a burst of balloons; a woman in her seventies snapping a picture of her eighty-year-old husband imitating the statue behind him; an American girl in blue jeans taking a picture of *another* American girl in blue jeans. Anybody and everybody, so long as they were taking a picture of somebody else. I felt like a Russian spy.

When we got back to the hotel that afternoon, I said, "Well, I guess you didn't have a chance to look for it. Taking all those pictures, I mean."

"I looked for it," he said.

"Did you find it?" I still had no idea what "it" was.

"Nope."

"Well, what are you going to do?"

"Look for it in Rome."

"Suppose you can't find it in Rome, either."

"I'll find it," he said.

"Meanwhile, can we go for a swim?"

"That's exactly what I want to do," he said.

"And maybe if Mommy takes a long time getting dressed, we can have a drink on the terrace together, and watch that man who's always fishing in the river."

The hotel had a little band there that evening, three pieces—piano, guitar, and drums. We sat in the outdoor garden, Mr. Stenner sipping at his Scotch on the rocks, and me sipping at the Florentine version of the Italian Shirley Temple. The drinks he ordered for me were different in each city. He simply asked the waiter for *"un' invenzione,"* and was always quick to add, *"Senza whisky,"* which meant, "Without whisky."

The Florentine invention without whisky looked like a rainbow. I'd never seen a more beautiful concoction in my entire life. It seemed a shame to drink it. I kept telling Mr. Stenner he should take a picture of it. But he didn't have his camera around his neck. He looked very nice and tanned, and very relaxed, and he kept tapping his hand on the table in time to the music the band was playing.

Something happened then that almost caused me to die of embarrassment.

A boy came over to the table.

He bowed from the waist.

In heavily accented English, he said, *"Mam'selle,* you prefer to dance?"

"What?" I said.

"*Voulez-vous danser avec moi?*" he said, and smiled. He looked about fourteen.

"He wants to dance, Abby," Mr. Stenner said.

"That is fine with you, *m'sieur?*" the boy said.

"It's up to Abby," Mr. Stenner said.

The boy was standing there, I could feel *him* getting more and more embarrassed with each passing minute, standing there like a dope with the sleeves of his sweater knotted around his neck, the sweater trailing down his back, the poor thing, standing there risking rejection!

So I nodded, and almost knocked my chair over when I got up.

His name was Henri Jacques.

Mr. Stenner later told me the boy was probably a famous American writer, since his name translated from the French as Henry James.

He was only thirteen. He told me that he lived in the town where Joan of Arc lifted the year-long English siege in 1429. He said if I ever came to France, I should look him up. He told me his father was the manager of a bank in Orléans. Then he asked me what *my* father did.

"He's an architect," I said.

"Ah," he said.

"And a photographer," I said.

"Ah," he said.

"In Italy, he's mostly a photographer."

"Ah," he said.

"Though in France once, he was an architect."

I was telling the truth.

Sort of.

After dinner, Mom and Mr. Stenner chatted with his parents, while Henri Jacques and I swung on the glider overlooking the river. The same man was down there fishing. He was always there in his boat whenever we came back from the city, sitting there all alone—boat, fisherman, and fishing pole reflecting in the water.

He never caught a fish all the while we were at that hotel.

"How old are you?" Henri Jacques asked.

"I'll be twelve next month." I said. "He's getting me a present that begins with an F," I said. "When we get to Rome. He hasn't found it yet."

"Something that begins with an F," Henri Jacques said.

"Mm," I said.

"Perhaps he buys you a Fiat," he said.

"What's a Fiat?" I said.

"An automobile," Henri Jacques said.

"I don't know how to drive," I said.

"You must learn, *non?*" Henri Jacques said, and shrugged.

13

When we got to Rome, Mr. Stenner told us he wanted to spend a few hours alone on the Via Condotti, and I immediately asked, "Are you going out to look for it?"

"Yes," he said.

"What is it? A Fiat?"

"A Fiat? That's an automobile," he said.

"Sure, I know. Are you buying me a car for my birthday?"

"Who'd drive it for you?" he asked, smiling.

"I thought maybe you could get me a chauffeur, too," I said, and giggled.

It was three days to my birthday.

When he got back to the hotel, he was whistling.

"You got it, didn't you?" I said.

"I got it," he said.

"What is it?"

He shook his head, and smiled, but I wouldn't give up. I kept poking and prodding and guessing and pleading, and on the day before my birthday, I finally found out what he'd bought me. We were on our way to the Villa Borghese. Mr. Stenner was driving the rented car, Mom was sitting beside him, and I was in the back.

"Is it a fake something?" I asked. "Is that what the F stands for? Like a fake diamond, or a fake . . ."

"No, it's very real," Mr. Stenner said. "And listen, Ab, I don't want to answer any more questions about it, okay? You'll find out tomorrow."

"Is it a fan? I saw some pretty fans in one of the shops yesterday."

"I'm not even going to answer you," he said. "Really, Ab. Even if you *do* guess what it is, I won't tell you."

"Well, *is* it a fan?"

"No, it's not a fan."

"Then is it a fife?"

"Abby," he said, "if you ask me one more question about that damn bracelet . . ."

He cut himself short.

He had said it. He had told me what it was.

There was a stunned moment of silence; he was realizing he'd told me, and I was realizing I'd spoiled my own surprise.

"A bracelet," I said.

He said nothing.

"But that doesn't start with a . . . oh, *I* get it," I said. "A forever."

He still said nothing.

"I'm sorry, Mr. Stenner," I said.

"I'm the one who should be sorry," he said.

"I shouldn't have kept pestering you that way."

"I shouldn't have slipped."

Mom looked first at him and then at me, and then she sighed.

When I woke up the next morning, there were 12s stuck to the ceiling all around my bed. Big 12s. They'd been made out of Italian newspapers, he'd cut up newspapers into 12s and Scotch-taped them to the ceiling like a canopy. There was a mild breeze coming through the window, the 12s flapped lazily. I was twelve years old. I shrieked in delight when I saw all those black-and-white 12s, and then I ran into the room next door without knocking and threw my arms around his neck and kissed him and said, "You made all those twelves, didn't you?"

"Not me," he said. "Must've been the concierge."

"The hall porter, you mean."

"Right, right, I keep forgetting what you call that guy downstairs. Did you see what's on the dresser?"

An envelope was propped up against a small box wrapped in gold paper. I knew what was in the box, of course. A bracelet. *That* much of it I'd managed to spoil. The card was in Italian. There was a little girl skipping rope on the front of it, and the words *Buon Compleanno, Mia Figlia.* I studied the card for a long time, trying to make out the Italian. Then at last, I said, "What does it say?"

"It says, 'Happy Birthday, Daughter.'"

I put the card down. I unwrapped the small package. The bracelet had three slender strands of something dark that looked like leather. They were fastened with thin gold strips to a thicker gold band behind them. It was the most beautiful thing I'd ever seen in my life.

"It's elephant hair," Mr. Stenner said. "It's supposed to bring good luck."

"Like a forever," I said.

"Yes."

"Thank you," I said. I went to Mom's little traveling kit and took the scissors from it, and carried it back to the bed where Mr. Stenner was sitting up against the pillow. I held out my wrist. I didn't have to say anything, he knew right off, same as I'd known when he was taking pictures of people taking pictures. He cut off the forever that I was wearing, and then slipped the new forever onto my wrist.

It meant something.

I was shaking.

It all began going beautifully after that.

The plan was to spend six days at Porto Santo Stefano, a peninsula off the coast, some ninety minutes north of Rome. Then we would drive back to Rome on the night before our departure, check in the rented car, spend the night in a hotel there, and taxi to the airport early the next morning. The hotel in Porto

Santo Stefano was one Mr. Stenner had stayed at before. On the day we arrived, we were sitting near the pool, Mom and Mr. Stenner drinking whisky-sodas, me drinking a silvery confection that looked like liquid mercury—when a woman suddenly said, "Peter?"

Mr. Stenner looked at her, and then jumped out of his chair. "Wenefride!" he said, and hugged the woman to him, and then kissed her on the cheek, and asked immediately, "Where's Emile? Is he here with you?"

"But of *course* he's here with me," the woman said, and laughed. She was in her early fifties, older than Mr. Stenner, and she glanced at Mom now with open curiosity.

"Wenefride," Mr. Stenner said, "let me introduce you to my wife and my daughter. Lillith, this is Wenefride Gastuche. Wenefride—Lillith and Abigail."

"How do you do?" Wenefride said, and extended her hand first to Mom and then to me. "Come, let's find Emile! He will be so happy to see you again."

The Gastuches were Belgians Mr. Stenner had met on his last trip to Italy. They didn't seem at all surprised that he and the former Mrs. Stenner were now divorced. ("I could sense it coming even then," Wenefride said to him.) I liked Wenefride a lot. You should have seen the stuff she had with her. She was only going to be away from home for two weeks, but she'd taken with her enough clothes to last eight months! That very afternoon, she showed me all the gowns and wigs and jewelry she'd brought, and it was like being in the best department store in the world. Her husband Emile was a little bald-headed man who was the director of a bank in Brussels. When he saw Mr. Stenner, he threw his arms around him and hugged him like a bear. In a minute, they were making plans. Emile said he had found a wonderful place to go swimming, and he told us to be ready at seven P.M. sharp, at which time he would personally drive us all there.

"You'll love it," he said, and waggled his eyebrows.

Mr. Stenner doubted very much that we'd enjoy swimming in the ocean after sunset, but Emile was a man of many surprises, and the spot he took us to was a thermal spa that bubbled up out of the ground and tumbled over a waterfall to dozens of little pools below. Sitting with Mr. Stenner in one of the pools, I said, "This is the best time I ever had," and then slid over the polished rocks to join Wenefride, where she was splashing in a pool some fifteen feet below.

Mom sat down beside Mr. Stenner.

"Are you happy?" he asked her.

"I'm very happy," she said. "Are you?"

"I'm very *very* happy."

"So am I!" I shouted up to them.

Mr. Stenner burst out laughing. "Do you know what I like best about you?" he shouted.

"What?" I shouted back.

"Your *ears!*"

The next night, Emile drove us to a rustic old inn high in the mountains. He got lost on the way there, and we didn't arrive till almost ten o'clock, but ahhh, what a feast! To start the meal, we had a breaded vegetable soup called *zuppa alla Certosina*. And then we ate fresh rock mullet in tomato sauce, and lamb roasted on a spit, and fried zucchini, and *funghi alla Fiorentina*, which were mushrooms prepared in the Florentine manner. The wine was delicious, the bread was hot and crisp. There was a blazing fire, and laughter from the kitchen, and laughter at the table, and I felt happier than I ever had in all my life.

In the morning, Mr. Stenner rented a fifty-one-foot ketch with a captain and two crew members and he took us and the Gastuches for a sail up the coast to a cove where we swam till noon, and ate sandwiches the hotel had made for us, and then dozed on the beach till the sun grew weak. He danced with Mom in the hotel lounge that night, and when he got back to the table, I said, "Aren't you going to dance with *me?*"

It was all going so damn beautifully.

Until, you know, I went and spoiled it again.

On the morning we were supposed to leave Porto Santo Stefano, I went into the room next door, and told Mom I wanted to talk to her privately. Mr. Stenner was still in bed, half-asleep. Mom was sitting at the dressing table, putting on her lipstick. I whispered in her ear.

She looked at me.

She put down her lipstick.

"I think you'd better discuss that with him," she said.

"*You* tell him," I said.

"Tell me what?" he asked, and raised himself up on one elbow.

"Never mind," I said.

"What is it?" he asked Mom.

"She wants to give you back the bracelet," Mom said.

"What?" he said.

"Before we go home. She doesn't want her father to see it. She's afraid it'll upset . . ."

"*What?*"

He got out of bed in his pajamas, and walked into the bathroom. I could hear the water running in there. Mom looked at me and shook her head. I went back to my own room. In a little while, I heard the door to their room opening and closing, and I peeked through my window and saw him walking down to the sea. I watched him. He went all the way to the edge of the ocean, and stood there on the rocks looking out at the deep blue cove. A sailboat was anchored just offshore, bobbing on the choppy water. The sky was overcast, the wind blowing fiercely. I saw him pull the shawl collar of his cardigan high on the back of his neck, and thrust his hands deep into his pockets. I put on one of his old sweaters over my long pink flannel nightgown. He'd given me the sweater a long time ago, it was the blue one with a hole eaten in it by Singapore the cat. I put on his leather hat, too, and pulled it down low on my forehead, almost hiding my eyes. Then I went out of the room.

He was climbing back up to the hotel when he saw me standing at the top of the winding steps cut into the rock ledge.

"Get back to the room," he said. "You'll catch cold."

"I'm sorry," I said.

"The hell with it," he said.

"Can't you tell I'm sorry?"

"No," he said.

"It's just . . ."

"Save it," he said, "I'm really not interested."

"It's just I have *two* of you, and it's hard. I don't want to hurt *either* of you, don't you see? I love you both."

"I don't believe you," he said.

"Oh, please believe me," I said. "I love you."

He told me later that he realized something in that instant. He realized that never in all the time he'd known me had he said those same words to *me*. I love you. I was only twelve, I was far too young to treat those words cheaply, they were to me treasured words. I love you. In Milan, Mom had asked him, *"Have you ever tried loving her?"* As he climbed those steps in Porto Santo Stefano, he wondered if he ever had.

I stood silhouetted against the sky. He climbed to where I was standing, and we looked at each other silently and solemnly, and then he put his arm around me, and together we began walking back to the hotel.

"I didn't mean to hurt you," I said.

"I know you didn't," he said. "Let's talk about it, okay?"

"Okay," I said. "And while we're talking, could we also figure out something else to call you? Because if you love somebody, you just can't go around calling him Mr. Stenner all the time. And I *do* love you. I wish you'd believe that. It makes me mad as hell when I tell you something, and you don't believe it."

"I believe it now," he said.

"That was my secret," I said. "Remember when I asked if you wanted to swap secrets? When you wouldn't tell me what my present was? Well, *that* was my secret. That I love you."

I stopped dead on the path, and looked up into his face. The cap was tilted low on my forehead, and my hair was blowing in the wind, sweeping across my face with each fresh gust. But I knew he could see my eyes clearly, and I only hoped he could read what was in them.

"I love you, too," he said.